"Have you heard who's back in town?"

a breathless voice behind Emily asked. "Nick O'Neill!"

"I don't know how he has the nerve to show his face in Mannington again," a second voice responded.

"The town bad boy and sweet Emily Carmichael were quite the item back in high school, weren't they?" another voice giggled. "How could anyone forget?"

The name Nick O'Neill broke through the smooth surface of Emily's day like a shark in a trout pond.

Registering the soccer-mom conversation taking place on the bleachers behind her, she struggled to keep her eyes on her twin sons' game.

Unfortunately, what she was seeing wasn't the third-graders. It was Nick's face, the way she'd last seen it, fourteen years ago. Angry, accusing…betrayed.

A familiar spasm of guilt caught her. Of all people, Nick O'Neill was coming back to town….

Books by Marta Perry

Love Inspired

A Father's Promise #41
Since You've Been Gone #75

MARTA PERRY

wanted to be a writer from the moment she encountered Nancy Drew, at about age eight. She didn't see publication of her stories until many years later, when she began writing children's fiction for Sunday school papers while she was a church educational director. Although now retired from that position in order to write full-time, she continues to play an active part in her church and loves teaching a lively class of fifth- and sixth-grade Sunday school students.

Marta lives in rural Pennsylvania with her husband of thirty-seven years and has three grown children. She loves to hear from readers and enjoys responding. She can be reached c/o Steeple Hill Books, 300 East 42nd Street, New York, NY 10017.

Since You've Been Gone
Marta Perry

Published by Steeple Hill Books™

STEEPLE HILL BOOKS

Steeple
Hill™

ISBN 0-373-87075-2

SINCE YOU'VE BEEN GONE

Copyright © 1999 by Martha Johnson

This edition published by arrangement with Steeple Hill Books.

® and TM are trademarks of Steeple Hill Books, used under license.
Trademarks indicated with ® are registered in the United States Patent
and Trademark Office, the Canadian Trade Marks Office and in other
countries.

Visit us at www.steeplehill.com

Printed in U.S.A.

Therefore, as God's chosen people, holy and dearly loved, clothe yourselves with compassion, kindness, humility, gentleness and patience. Bear with each other and forgive whatever grievances you may have against one another. Forgive as the Lord forgave you. And over all these virtues put on love, which binds them all together in perfect unity.
—*Colossians* 3:12-14

This book is dedicated to my parents,
Joe and Florence Perry,
with love and gratitude.
And, as always, to Brian.

Chapter One

Emily Carmichael's twin sons raced down the soccer field, David struggling to keep up with Trey as he always did. David's jersey had come out of his shorts, flapping around his knees like a skirt, and his glasses slid down his nose. The soccer ball rolled toward him, dazzling white against green.

"Kick it, David. Kick it!" Trey shouted.

Emily held her breath. Just this once, if David could only succeed…

He swung his leg, missed and sprawled on the turf, his glasses flying.

Emily's nails bit into her palms. She couldn't run to him, no matter how much her heart ached. That would violate the macho code of third-grade boys. The ball and the players surged on toward the goal, leaving him behind. Trey ran a few steps, hesitated, then turned and came back to his brother. Emily breathed again as he helped David up.

"At least you won't have to get him a new pair of glasses. Looks like Trey found them."

Emily turned to smile at Lorna Moore. "That would only be the fourth time this year."

"One of the costs of sports they don't tell you about when you sign your kids up."

A golden leaf from the trees that fringed the field drifted into Emily's lap. She held it for a moment, mind absently registering the soccer mom conversation taking place around her…car pools, school schedules, dancing lessons…

"Have you heard?" a breathless voice behind her asked. "You know who's back in town? Nick O'Neill!"

Emily's fingers tightened, crumpling the leaf. The name broke through the smooth surface of her day like a shark in a trout pond.

She struggled to keep her face impassive, her eyes on the game. Unfortunately, what she was seeing wasn't the group of eight-year-olds. It was Nick's face the way she'd last seen it fourteen years ago— angry, accusing, betrayed. The familiar spasm of guilt caught her.

"I don't know how he has the nerve to show his face in Mannington again."

The comment floated through the autumn air, pitched just loudly enough to reach Emily. Sooner or later someone would ask her directly. They were too intimidated to question her father-in-law, so they'd ask her.

James Carmichael, benevolent dictator of Carmichael Mills, major employer in this small Pennsylvania town, was enough to intimidate anyone. He ruled his mill the way he'd once ruled his son and now tried to rule his son's widow. Only economic necessity had forced him to consider sharing his power through the merger with Ex Corp.

Emily brushed the remnants of the leaf from her tan slacks. Since Jimmy's death four years ago, she'd taken his seat on the mill's board of directors, not that her formidable father-in-law allowed anyone else to do much directing. At least he kept her informed about company business...in this case, that Nick O'Neill, of all people, was coming to town as Ex Corp's representative.

"Well, Emily, aren't you going to tell us? Is it true that Nick O'Neill is back?" Margaret Wentworth leaned forward to rest an elegant hand on Emily's lawn chair, the slightest hint of malice glinting in her eyes.

She should have known it would be Margaret who asked. Wentworths had lived in Mannington almost as long as Carmichaels had, and Margaret had once believed Jimmy Carmichael was hers for the taking.

Emily tried to smile. "Ex Corp is sending him to manage the merger with the mill. I don't know any more than that."

"You mean you haven't seen him yet?" Margaret's arched brows lifted. "My husband saw him walking down Elm Street just this morning."

Please don't let her bring up the past, Lord. Please. It's buried, isn't it?

"We thought perhaps he was coming to see you. You're such old friends." Margaret planted the barb and smiled.

"I haven't seen him." That almost sounded as if she cared. "He'll probably be too busy with the merger to look up old acquaintances."

"Not just acquaintances. You and Nick were quite the item back in high school, weren't you?" Margaret laughed lightly. "The town bad boy and sweet little Emily, the doctor's daughter. How could anyone forget that?"

The smile felt as stiff as cardboard on Emily's face. She could almost hear the indrawn breaths as everyone waited for her response. "I'm sure people have better things to do than worry about people I forgot a long time ago. Do you remember all your old boyfriends, Margaret?"

Anger flashed in Margaret's eyes. Emily bit her lip. She hadn't meant it as a reference to Jimmy. She considered apologizing, then realized that would make matters worse.

Margaret turned away with a brittle laugh, and Emily's hands unclenched. Apparently she'd been kidding herself. Memories were long in a town like Mannington. They certainly stretched back fourteen years.

Guilt flickered again. Her past was returning to

haunt her, in the shape of the man she'd never forgotten.

What was she thinking? Of course she'd forgotten Nick. And would again. He'd be here for a few weeks, and then he'd leave and everything would return to normal.

A little shiver went down her spine. She knew why Nick was supposedly coming to Mannington. But given what had happened between him and the town—between him and Emily—she couldn't believe that was his only reason.

The whistle blew, ending the game, and the twins rushed toward her. She shoved thoughts of Nick's return to the back of her mind and stood to meet them.

"Good game, guys." She ruffled Trey's hair, put a hand on David's shoulder.

"We almost won, Mom." Trey, ever the optimist, gave her the grin that one day would break girls' hearts. "Next time we'll do it."

"Next time we have to play the Tigers," David pointed out. "They're a lot better than we are." He kicked disconsolately at a clump of grass, and Emily knew he was seeing the ball he'd missed.

"Well, we just have to get better." Trey said it as if nothing could be easier. "When we get home, we'll practice. You'll see. Everything's going to be great."

For an instant, Emily envied him his optimism. She'd like to feel that way about the changes Nick O'Neill and this merger might bring to town.

No, that was impossible. But it should be possible,

even easy, to avoid the apprehension roused by the thought of seeing him. She just had to avoid seeing him at all.

Nick leaned back in his chair, stretching, and rested his hands on the papers he'd been studying. He'd been a long time putting himself in a position of power over Carmichael Mills. Now that he'd gotten here, he fully intended to savor it.

He frowned down at the file on his desk. Preliminary, and way too sketchy. When he met with James Carmichael, he'd demand a full accounting. And for once in his life, Carmichael wouldn't be able to call the shots. Nick would enjoy that moment. He needed to prepare, but concentrating proved difficult.

Sound drifted through the window—kids' voices, somewhere outside. He could have been isolated from that if he'd chosen to stay in a motel, but that wasn't the way he'd wanted to come back to Mannington, staying in a cheap motel room like a traveling salesman.

For a lot of years he'd imagined returning. He'd pictured himself walking into one of the big houses on Elm or Sycamore, the kind of place where he hadn't been welcomed fourteen years ago.

He shook his head at the ridiculous dream. But he couldn't deny the pleasure he'd felt at leasing the old Findley house, fully furnished, for his stay.

The window he'd opened to let in some crisp autumn air was also letting in what sounded like World

War III. Only two kids, by the voices, but they made enough noise for twenty. He'd have to close the window.

The curtain billowed, and a soccer ball flew through the window, bouncing twice on the Findleys' Oriental rug.

That generated silence outside. Nick reached for the ball, rolling it across the carpet, and listened.

"You kicked it. You go get it." The speaker was young and male.

"I'm not going in." Equally young and male, but scared.

"Well, somebody has to. We can't leave a brand new soccer ball in there. Besides, it has our initials on it."

Nick flipped the ball over. A childish hand had printed a *D* and a *T* in black marker next to the logo. He grinned, half-expecting a small figure to bounce through the window next.

"Can't we ask Mommy to do it?"

"Mom said to leave the new neighbor alone." It sounded as if the speaker took a deep breath. "All right, David. I'll do it. You boost me up."

Nick reached the window just as a small figure wobbled precariously against the sill, some four feet off the ground.

"Looking for this?" He held up the ball.

A pair of brown eyes focused on him, then widened alarmingly. The boy—no, boys, one on the other's shoulders—swayed backward, about to fall into the

Findleys' azalea bush. Nick lunged through the open window and grabbed the kid just as he fell.

"You okay?" He leaned across the sill, setting the boy onto the grass, then glanced from one to the other. And did a double take. Twins—identical twins Both looking at him with scared brown eyes. He grinned. "It's all right. I don't bite. Are you okay?"

"Yes, sir." The window climber got his composure back first. "I—we're sorry. We didn't think anybody was home."

"We just wanted our ball." The other one's voice trembled.

"This ball, you mean, David?" He ventured a guess that David wasn't the window climber and got a scared, awestruck look in return. "How do I know it's yours?"

"I—I—because…" He ran out of steam.

The other one grinned. "He's kidding, David. He knows it's ours. We're the only ones here."

Nick flipped the ball around. "Okay, I guess *D* is for David. What's *T* stand for? Timmy?"

The boy shook his head. "Trey." He straightened, holding out a small, rather dirty hand. "James Allen Carmichael the Third. Only, everybody calls me Trey."

James Allen… These were Emily's kids, staring at him with Emily's golden brown, vulnerable eyes.

For an instant he couldn't say anything at all. Then he realized the boy was still holding his hand out. He shook hands gravely, first with Trey, then with David.

"Nice to meet you. I'm Nick O'Neill."

The name didn't seem to mean anything to them. The old man must have told Emily he was coming, but she obviously hadn't mentioned it to her sons. Well, why should she? He was ancient history as far as she was concerned.

Just as she was to him. He wasn't the kid he'd been fourteen years ago, and Emily Forrest—no, Carmichael—didn't mean a thing to him. Not one single thing. The score he'd come back to Mannington to settle was with the old man, not her.

"Are you a friend of Professor Findley?" David had apparently decided Nick wasn't a monster waiting to eat soccer balls and unfortunate little boys.

"Not exactly. I'm just renting his house while he's away. Do you two live around here?"

"Over there." Trey pointed across the back lawn. "Our backyard bumps into this one. Professor Findley didn't care if we ran in his yard sometimes."

David nudged his twin. "Only when he wasn't home. That's what he said. Only when he wasn't home."

"Well, he isn't home, is he?" Trey planted his hands on his hips and glared at his twin.

"N-no." David frowned. "But Mommy said not to bother the new neighbor."

"We're not bothering him, exactly." Trey smiled at Nick. "Are we bothering you?"

"The soccer ball..." David apparently served as conscience for both of them.

"That's okay." Nick tossed the ball out the window to them. "Tell you what. How about if I come out and kick the ball around with you? I could use a break."

Trey's eyes lit up. "Would you?"

"We're not exactly *good*," David added.

Actually, Nick should be planning his meeting with Carmichael. But the lure of seeing Emily's boys a bit more was irresistible. He shoved the sweet, heart-shaped face out of his mind. She'd be a woman now, not the girl he remembered—the girl who'd let him down and broken his too-susceptible seventeen-year-old heart.

Nick swung his legs over the sill and ducked under the sash.

"Are you coming out the window?" Trey blinked at him.

"Why not?" He dropped lightly to the ground in the Findleys' flower bed.

David eyed him. "Mostly grown-ups don't climb out windows."

"Why do you suppose that is?"

Trey shrugged. "'Cause people would talk about them, I guess."

People will talk. Yes, he definitely was back in Mannington again. Emily had used that phrase to put up barriers between them more than once. It had been years since he'd felt the urge to do something just so people would talk, but he felt that way now. The town had that effect on him.

"Will people talk about me playing soccer with you?"

Trey looked doubtful. "Maybe."

"Good. Let's do it." He grabbed the ball. "Bet I can dribble clear to that lilac bush before you can steal the ball."

He started across the grass, weaving through fallen leaves no one had raked, the boys racing after him. He didn't make it halfway before Trey, face intent, eyes narrowed, ducked in front of him and swiped the ball away. Looked like it had been too many years since he'd had time for a game of soccer.

He chased Trey and the ball, managed to steal it, lost it again when David charged into him. For several minutes they dodged each other across the grass. Crisp autumn air chilled his throat, stiff muscles came alive and a nearly forgotten exhilaration surged through him.

Kids probably felt like this all the time. They hadn't gotten so busy that play turned into exercise, one more chore to fit into an impossible day.

Trey wasn't skilled, but he was fast, stealing the ball and grinning. David tried valiantly, but he couldn't seem to coordinate running and kicking. Maybe it was the glasses that kept sliding down his nose. Nick resisted the urge to push them back up for him.

"I got it, I got it!"

Trey ducked around him, shouting. David went for the ball and barreled into Nick's legs. He tried to untangle himself, lost his balance and saw the ground coming at him. The three of them ended in a breathless heap, dry leaves rustling.

"I didn't know tackling was part of soccer."

He looked up at the sound of her voice. She stood between him and the sun, and light streaked her soft brown hair with gold.

His breath caught in his throat, as if he'd been hit by a three-hundred-pound tackle instead of a small boy. The depth of his astonishment stunned him. In all his plans for what would happen when he came back to Mannington, he'd left something important out of the reckoning. He hadn't thought he'd feel anything when he saw Emily again.

Emily's heart seemed to be beating somewhere up in her throat. It was a wonder she'd gotten the words out at all, let alone that they'd had just the right casual, unshaken tone.

She had a crazy desire to laugh. No, she could hardly convince herself she wasn't shaken by seeing Nick O'Neill again.

Remnants—that's all the feelings were that flooded her. Bits and pieces of memories she thought she'd forgotten had surfaced, but she could control them. She could be just as cool and detached as she'd promised herself she'd be if she ran into Nick.

Nick disentangled himself from the twins and rolled to his feet. Tall, muscular, a stranger. Not much there of the boy she'd once known. They were meeting again as old acquaintances, that was all.

He looked down at her, those incredibly dark blue eyes unsmiling. "It's been a long time." He held out his hand, and for the life of her, she couldn't move. His mouth twitched. "Or were you thinking it hasn't been long enough?"

"No, no, of course not. It's nice to see you again, Nick." She put her hand in his, felt his fingers curve warmly around hers. Her palm tingled for an instant.

Nick's dark, winged brows lifted. Black Irish, that was what people had said he was, hair like black silk contrasting with the deep, deep blue of his eyes.

"Is it nice to see me? Somehow I have the feeling that Mannington doesn't exactly welcome the returning prodigal."

"You're not exactly that, are you?" She drew her hand away, pulling her polite, social manner around her like a cloak. "I don't think you can blame people for being a little apprehensive. No one understands exactly what this merger might mean to the town." Surely he remembered how rumors flew in a one-industry town. Would the merger bring prosperity or layoffs? No one was sure, and everyone cared.

"Only natural for people to be a little distant?" Something faintly mocking showed in the curve of his mouth. "No lingering prejudice against me, for old times' sake?"

The words she'd overheard at the soccer game flashed through her mind. People still thought of Nick as the rebellious, angry boy who'd left town under a cloud. They wouldn't be easily convinced by the cool, composed armor he wore now.

"I'm sure no one even—" She stopped, unable to produce a polite social lie with his skeptical gaze on her and very aware of the twins watching, eyes wide.

His smile turned a shade warmer. "Some things never change. Sweet Emily still can't say a bad word about anyone, can she?"

She felt her cheeks warm, although why it should be an insult to be called sweet she didn't know. "You'll find lots of things have changed," she said, evading the personal comment.

"Not you." His eyes swept her. "You still look about fifteen."

She glanced down, realizing she wore her oldest jeans and a tattered sweatshirt. Why, oh why, did he have to catch her this way? She'd intended their meeting, if there had to be one, to take place at the mill, in a pleasant, professional arena where it would be easy to remind herself that she was a grown woman.

She forced a smile. "I see you've met my boys." And what was he doing in her yard, anyway, playing with her sons? She stifled a ridiculous impulse to send the boys inside, as if they needed protecting.

"Yes, we've met." Nick grinned at what seemed to be a warning look from Trey. The twins had been up to something, obviously. "I'm renting the Findley house while I'm here. The boys were showing me how much I've forgotten about soccer."

"I thought football was your game." The words brought a sudden vivid image of Nick, grinning and triumphant after a touchdown, searching the stands for her. She remembered meeting his gaze, almost speechless with joy that, of all the girls who'd yearned for him, he'd chosen her.

"You played football?" Trey's face lit up. That was his dream, one she kept trying to redirect into something that seemed safer. "What position?"

"Wide receiver." Nick shook his head. "I was a lot faster in those days."

"Wow. Could you..."

"Trey." She would stop that before it started. "Mr. O'Neill is here on business. He doesn't have time for games."

Nick's eyebrows lifted. "How do you know what I have time for?" His eyes teased her in a way that was so familiar, it captured her breath.

He'd looked at her like that before, said something very like that the first time they'd talked, when she'd come shyly up to him after football practice, assigned to get an interview for the school paper, sure he'd brush her off, or worse, think she was like the other girls who made excuses to talk to him.

"I...well, I don't, but I assumed Ex Corp didn't send you here to play soccer." *Remember why he's here. Don't let the past interfere.*

"They like their executives to stay fit. Don't you think I can use the exercise?" His eyes, half laughing, half challenging, dared her to assess him.

"I'm sure you can get a temporary membership at the gym," she said primly, trying not to notice the way his white sweater clung to his broad shoulders.

"But this is much more fun, Emily." His gaze warmed and his voice lowered on her name as if they were the only ones present.

Her blood seemed to be singing through her veins, and there must be something wrong with her vision, because she couldn't separate the man he was now from the boy she'd once loved.

The man's emotions seemed kept under tight rein, as if they couldn't be trusted in polite society, but she still saw signs of the boy—reckless, heedless, appealing. She didn't think he'd changed all that much, except that *appealing* wasn't the word any longer. *Dangerously attractive* said it better.

She took a steadying breath, then looked at her sons. All right. Nick might have awakened memories of the girl who'd once loved him, but she intended never to be that vulnerable again. And if that meant turning herself inside out to avoid him while he was here, that's what she'd do.

"Time to get washed up for supper, boys. Thank Mr. O'Neill for playing with you."

Trey grimaced, then held out his hand in the formal manner his grandfather insisted upon. "Thank you, sir."

"It was fun," David added. Then her shy son startled her by grinning at Nick as if they were old friends. "Come play with us again."

Nick shot her a look that said he knew exactly how little that pleased her. "I'll try." He smiled. "If your mother says it's okay."

"Mommy..."

Emily shooed them toward the kitchen. "We'll see. Go on now."

When they'd gone inside, she turned back to Nick, to be met with a skeptical look.

"We'll see? Was that what your father said fourteen years ago when he found out you were dating me?"

The memory of the confrontation with her father still hurt, but she had no intention of letting Nick know that.

"It was so long ago, I'm afraid I don't remember." She held out her hand with a formality that would have met with her father-in-law's approval. "It was nice seeing you, Nick. Maybe we'll meet again while you're in town."

The warmth of his grip made her doubt the wisdom of the gesture. He smiled, his fingers curling around hers. "Oh, I'm sure we will."

She tugged her hand free. "You'll be busy with the negotiations."

"Aren't you a member of the board of directors?" His tone suggested he wasn't too impressed.

"That doesn't mean much where my father-in-law is concerned. I'm sure he's the one you'll be dealing with."

"Really?" His dark brows lifted. "That's not the impression he gave me."

She could only stare at him. "What do you mean?"

"I talked to Carmichael on the phone earlier." Nick paused. "He said he planned to deputize you to give me the grand tour of the mill and see that I have what I need. According to him, we're going to be spending a lot of time together." He smiled, a hint of mockery in his eyes. "It'll be just like old times, Emily."

Chapter Two

The shock in Emily's eyes took Nick by surprise. Apparently she hadn't known what Carmichael planned. Suspicion blossomed quickly. What exactly was that crafty old man plotting? Did Carmichael think he could somehow turn the long-ago relationship between his daughter-in-law and Nick to his advantage?

His mouth tightened. If Carmichael thought that, he was wrong. There was nothing left of those feelings, nothing but a minor resentment for the way Emily and he had parted. He was past the age to be nursing a broken heart over something that happened so many years ago.

He forced a smile. "I take it Carmichael didn't confide in you."

"No." Her smile looked just as forced as his. "I'm sorry, but I—" She stopped, absently snapping a dead flower head from the chrysanthemums and then looking up at him. "If you remember him at all, you'll remember that James Carmichael likes to run things his own way."

Remember? Oh yes, he remembered, all right. "Even with his son's widow?"

Her smile took on a rueful tinge. "Especially with his son's widow." She shook her head. "I'll talk to him. I'm sure this is something he should do himself. He can't expect me—" She broke off the sentence, those golden brown eyes distressed.

"To work with an old boyfriend?" He finished for her.

She brushed a strand of hair back from her face, fingers tangling in it. All in an instant he remembered how her hair felt, silky strands as fine as a baby's curling around his fingers.

Whoa, back off. He wasn't a kid anymore, and he wasn't going that route again. And he certainly wouldn't let a few raw memories distract him from what he'd come to Mannington to do.

"I doubt he even knows we once dated." Emily sounded as if she was trying to convince herself. "I'm just not the best person for the job, and this merger is important not only to us, but to the whole town."

She looked so upset that he found himself wanting to do or say anything to wipe that expression from her face.

"It's okay, Emily." He resisted the impulse to stroke the frown from between her brows. "I'll talk to Carmichael. You're too busy with those boys of yours to spend the next month shepherding me around.''

The troubled look faded from her eyes as she glanced toward the house, her expression softening. ''They do keep me busy.''

He followed the direction of her gaze. A porch stretched across the back of the white Victorian, looking as if it badly needed a fresh coat of paint. It was cluttered with bikes, bats and other kid stuff. The twins had left the back door open, and the noise of a lively altercation floated out.

''Sounds like they need a full-time referee.''

''They squabble constantly.'' She shook her head. ''I keep telling myself it's their age. But if anyone else dares to pick on one of them, they merge in an instant.''

The intensity of the love in her voice rattled him. She hadn't changed—that had been his first thought—but now he realized it wasn't true.

The girl he'd left behind had been tentative, vulnerable, with an eagerness to please everyone shining in those golden-brown eyes. She'd matured into a woman—soft, strong, assured. Probably the only place she was still vulnerable was in her love for her sons.

She was looking at him, and he had to say something. ''They're nice kids. Look a lot like you, don't they?''

She smiled. "Everyone says so. I see Jimmy in them a bit."

He didn't want to remember how he'd felt when he learned she'd married Jimmy, his one-time friend. "I was sorry to hear about his death."

"Thank you." Emotion darkened her eyes for just a moment. "It's been a long time, I guess. Over four years."

"Do the twins remember him?" *Do you still grieve for him, Emily?*

She shrugged. "Little flashes of memory, I guess. They don't really talk about it much. For them, it was half their lifetimes ago."

"I suppose they're a real comfort to Carmichael."

"I..." She looked wary suddenly. "Yes, I guess so. He's never been the bouncing-them-on-his-knee sort of grandparent, though."

He tried to picture that rigid autocrat in the role and failed utterly. "No, I guess he wouldn't be." As he remembered it, Jimmy had been scared to death of his father, always trying nervously to live up to the old man's expectations and failing most of the time.

Emily bent to pick up the gardening gloves and trowel she must have abandoned when he'd invaded her space. A warm flush mounted her cheeks. "I shouldn't have said that. He's fond of the boys. And pleased that there's a James Carmichael the Third to carry on the name."

Then it hit him. The cost of his revenge would be higher than he'd anticipated, and it was one Emily and her children would pay. If he succeeded in what he'd come to Mannington to do, there wouldn't be a mill for Trey and David to inherit.

He pushed the thought away with a spurt of anger. This didn't have anything to do with Emily's kids. Jimmy had undoubtedly left them very well provided for. In the long run, this didn't have anything to do with the old man's money, either. The revenge he had in mind would hit James Carmichael where it hurt, in his pride and in his power.

Emily glanced toward the house again. "It sounds as if I'd better get in there and calm things down." She hesitated, then smiled. "It was good to see you again, Nick."

That smile swept right through him, riding a surge of memories. He wanted...

Before he could move or speak, she turned and was gone, crossing the back porch, the screen door slamming behind her. He had to suppress the urge to follow her.

Frowning, he started back across the lawn. He'd have to work harder at shutting down his feelings. Remembering Emily the way she'd been—worse, being attracted to Emily the way she was now—didn't fit into his plans at all.

He had to concentrate on his business with Carmichael. And probably the only way he could accomplish that was to stay as far away from Emily as possible.

He kicked at the soccer ball the twins had forgotten, then tossed it toward the house. It shouldn't be that hard to steer clear of Emily, not since she obviously wanted exactly the same thing.

"Macaroni and cheese!" Trey shouted, running into the kitchen from a trip to the bathroom to, Emily hoped, wash his hands.

"I love macaroni and cheese, Mommy." David slid onto his chair, his expression blissful.

She suppressed a twinge of guilt over taking the easy way out when it came to supper. She'd been too distracted after that unexpected encounter with Nick to be creative in the kitchen.

"David, it's your turn to ask the blessing."

The three of them joined hands around the table, and Emily's heart warmed at the feel of those little hands in hers. *Lord, help me to be the parent they need.* Her silent prayer added to David's recitation of the blessing. *Guide me to do the right things for them.* Nick's face flickered in her mind. *And help me to—*

She stopped, biting her lip. To what? It hardly seemed right to ask God to help her avoid Nick.

"Amen," David said.

"Macaroni!" Trey scooped up the serving dish before his brother could reach it. He sniffed the aroma, smiling.

"Vegetables, too," she warned, passing him the green beans.

He gave her a serious look. "Are you sure macaroni isn't a vegetable?"

"Positive." She wouldn't let herself smile. Trey was too quick to take advantage of his ability to charm her. In that, he was very like Jimmy.

"I like him," David said around a mouthful of macaroni.

She glanced at him, startled, then realized he was talking about Nick. She suppressed a sigh. It would be too much to hope they'd forget so entrancing a new friend quickly.

"Was Nick a good football player, Mom?" Trey looked thoughtfully at the lone green bean on his fork.

"Mr. O'Neill," she corrected.

"He said we could call him Nick."

"He came out the window," David said breathlessly.

For an instant she could only stare at him. "What?"

"He came out the window. When we…" David stopped, obviously struck by the realization that he was heading in a dangerous direction.

"Blabbermouth," Trey muttered.

"All right, out with it." Emily put her fork down. "Exactly how did you meet Mr. O'Neill?"

David's lower lip began to tremble. "We didn't mean…"

"We were kicking the soccer ball. Practicing so we'll get better, like you said we should." Trey's voice was filled with a righteousness that made her instantly suspicious. "We couldn't help it."

"Where exactly did the soccer ball go?"

Trey drew a circle in his macaroni. "You know the window in the Findleys' den?"

"Trey! You didn't break a window!" What an introduction that was for Nick...but she should be a lot more worried about the Findleys' window.

He shook his head. "It was open, and the ball just popped in."

"We didn't mean to, Mommy," David added.

She closed her eyes for a moment. Well, it could have been worse. She opened them. "I hope you apologized."

"We did," Trey said quickly. "He said it was okay. Then he said he'd play ball with us."

"And he came out the window," David said again.

That had obviously made an impression on David. She could only hope he wouldn't try to imitate Nick's behavior.

"Was that—" She hesitated. She didn't want to pump her sons. On the other hand, she really wanted to know something. "Was that before he knew who you were, or after?"

Trey frowned, as if trying to remember.

"After," David said. "Remember, Trey, we talked about our initials on the ball, and he asked our names."

"After," Trey agreed. "You didn't answer, Mom. Was he a good football player?"

"Very good." She could almost hear the cheers. "I remember there was talk of a big college scholarship for him."

"Where did he go? Who did he play for?" Trey's eyes rounded.

"He...didn't." She shook her head, trying not to remember those last few painful days. "He moved away."

"But didn't he still play football?"

Most of the time she thought Trey's persistence was a good quality. Not now. She got up, carrying her plate to the sink, suddenly not hungry.

"I don't know, Trey. We lost touch after that." Lost touch. What a nice way of putting it. "Get busy eating now. I know you both have spelling words to work on. I want to hear you practicing."

An hour later the dishes were done, and the sound of a spelling drill issued from the twins' bedroom, interrupted by sporadic giggles. Emily walked slowly into her own room, then closed the door.

The back window, with its ruffled white Cape Cods, looked out toward the Findley house. She stood for a moment, staring out. Then, feeling a little ridiculous, she pulled the shade.

The small box was in the back of her sweater drawer in the double dresser. She felt for it, then pulled it out and lifted the lid.

Nick's class ring. She picked it up. The gold was still bright after all these years, the letters still sharp and clear. Why not? It had hardly been worn. Nick had given it to her the night of the autumn dance. And the next night—

She closed her eyes against the memory, but it wouldn't go away...

"I told you that boy was no good." Her father had been ready to leave for an evening call at the hospital, doctor's bag in his hand. He'd paused at the door, then come back to touch her shoulder lightly, pity mixing with the anger in his eyes. "I'm sorry, Emily. Sorry you had to be hurt by this."

She shook her head, unable to speak, her throat choked with tears. Then she managed to get the words out. "But nobody's proved Nick was involved. You can't blame him."

"Flynn O'Neill is a thief." Her father's hand tightened on her shoulder. "Somebody else had to be involved. He couldn't have pulled it off alone. Who would it be but the son? They haven't been in town long enough to involve anyone else."

"Nick wouldn't..." Fresh tears stopped the words.

He sighed. "Emily, I don't have time for this now. Those O'Neills should consider themselves lucky Mr. Carmichael agreed to let them leave town again, instead of pressing charges against them."

He started for the door, then turned back once more. "I want your promise, you hear? Promise me you won't speak to that boy again." His face darkened. "Bad enough that everyone in town knows you were dating him. Don't make things worse for either of us."

A doctor's family had to be above rumor, above

scandal. That had been drilled into her from the time she could talk.

"I promise, Daddy."

"Good girl."

Usually those words soothed her. That time they hadn't worked.

Her father had gone then, leaving her to her tears. But that hadn't been the end, not that night. There had been worse to come. She twisted the ring in her fingers.

"Emily, you can't believe this!" Nick had stood on the back porch, in the shadows, hand pressed against the screen door, the rasp of crickets forming a chorus behind his words.

"Please." Emily sent an apprehensive glance across the lawn. "My father made me promise not to talk to you. If anyone sees us I'll get in trouble."

He slapped his palm against the door frame, his lean face angry and frustrated. "Come out and listen, then. You don't have to talk. Come out or I'll make enough noise that the whole neighborhood will know I'm here."

She felt like a badminton birdie, swatted back and forth between two rackets. Her father, Nick... She shoved the door open and slipped onto the porch. "Only for a minute...."

The fierce pressure of Nick's mouth cut off the words. For a moment she resisted, then her arms went around him just as fiercely. She clung to the hard strength of his shoulders. She couldn't let him go; she couldn't!

When his mouth lifted, his face was as tear-wet as hers.

"Nick." Her voice trembled. "You didn't do it, did you? I know you didn't."

His hands grasped her shoulders, fingers biting. "I'm no thief. And neither is my dad. You ought to know that!"

"I do, I know it." Even as she said the words, doubt flickered in her mind. Oh, not about Nick, never about Nick. But what did she know about Flynn O'Neill? That he looked angry, that he scared her a little the one time she'd met him, that people said he was a transient, a troublemaker...

Maybe Nick sensed what she didn't say. He held her away from him, eyes darkening. "Do you know? Are you sure about me?"

"Nick! Of course I'm sure!" She pulled his hand to her lips, pressing a kiss against it. "I know you'd never steal."

He drew her back against him, and his breath was hot across her cheek. "Then go with me. Now, tonight. I can't lose you, Emily. I love you."

"Go...go with you?" Her mind could hardly comprehend it.

"My dad's headed for New York, but we don't have to go with him." Nick's words gained momentum, as if they could carry her along on the tide of his energy. "We can go to Maryland. We can get married there. I'll get a job, I'll take care of you."

"Married." She hardly heard the rest of it. Run away with Nick, leave her father to face the gossip, the sly looks...

Nick caught her chin, forcing her to look at him. Slowly, so slowly, she saw his love die, drowning in the deep blue of his eyes.

"You do believe it."

"No!"

His mouth twisted bitterly. "Last night you said you loved me. I thought you were the one person in this crummy town I could count on. Or did you just want this?"

He snatched the class ring she wore on a chain around her neck. The fragile links pressed coldly on her skin and then snapped, the ring coming away in Nick's hand.

"Don't!"

She reached for him, but it was too late. He spun away from her, flinging the ring across the lawn.

"Your ring..."

"I don't want it." His gaze was contemptuous. "Just like I don't want you. You're like all the rest of this town. Have a nice life, Emily."

Before she could speak the light came on in Mrs. Dailey's kitchen next door. She sent a scared glance that way, sure she'd see old Mrs. Dailey peering out between the lace curtains, but no one was there.

She turned back to Nick, tears choking her, but

he'd gone, cutting across the dark lawn the way he'd run down the lighted football field.

And now he was back. Emily looked soberly at herself in the dresser mirror, then down at the ring in her hand. Nick didn't know she still had it, of course. He probably wouldn't believe that she'd spent hours that night on her hands and knees in the wet grass with a flashlight, the search made more difficult by the tears clouding her vision. Well, he never would know.

Guilt swept over her again, familiar guilt. Oh, not that she hadn't gone with him. That would have been wrong. They'd been way too young—too young to have any sense of what marriage involved. But some-how...

She shook her head for the girl she'd been. She'd let him go away thinking she'd turned against him, too, just like the rest of the town. She'd hurt him, and the memory of that still had the power to make her ashamed.

But it was too late to mend that with Nick now. He wouldn't believe her, and if he did, he wouldn't care.

If she'd learned anything from the feelings Nick had roused, just by seeing him again, it was that she couldn't afford the emotional cost of being around him. And that meant she had to talk to her father-in-law as soon as possible. She had to convince him that she was the last person in the world who should be put in charge of Nick's visit to Carmichael Mills.

Chapter Three

"It will just be a moment, Mrs. Carmichael." Martha Rand, James Carmichael's longtime secretary, gave Emily a cool smile across the desk that barricaded the inner sanctum at Carmichael Mills.

They'd known each other for years, but once Emily had become Mrs. Carmichael it hadn't occurred to Martha to call her anything else.

She smiled back, repressing the urge the woman gave her to be sure her hair was neat and her blouse tucked in. "I'm not in a hurry."

She wandered across acres of broadloom to the wall of photographs that made a focal point in the outer office. At least, she wasn't in any hurry as long as she saw her father-in-law this morning. Saw him and convinced him that someone else had to take on the job of escorting Nick O'Neill through the coming weeks.

A mostly sleepless night had convinced her of the wisdom of avoiding Nick for the rest of his stay. Incredible, to think seeing him after all these years could spin her emotions just as he had fourteen years ago. Maybe her instincts told her that, in spite of his sophisticated veneer, Nick was still a restless, reckless wanderer, just like his father.

Incredible, too, to realize that half the people in town remembered her relationship with Nick, and that still more identified him, however hazily, with the theft from the mill. The series of phone calls she'd fielded the evening before had shown her that.

Oh, no one had come right out and asked for the gossip on Nick O'Neill's return, or asked how she was taking it. The variety of excuses for calling had been remarkable, but that's all they'd been—excuses.

People cared, she told herself. Cared about her, cared about her boys and cared about the future of this town.

She focused on the turn-of-the-century photograph of the original mill, with Jimmy's grandfather standing in front of his workers, the red brick mill looming protectively behind them. That image symbolized what the mill meant to all of them. Without the mill, Mannington might just dry up and blow away.

"Mr. Carmichael will see you now, Mrs. Carmichael."

If Martha Rand heard anything strange about that sentence, she didn't indicate it. Emily nodded to her, grasped the gleaming brass knob and pushed open the door to the private office.

Her father-in-law, rising behind the massive mahogany desk, inclined his head with a hint of a frosty smile. "Good morning, Emily."

"Good morning." Entering this room always made her feel the same as she did entering the principal's office or being hailed by a policeman—sure she'd done nothing wrong, but vaguely guilty anyway.

James Carmichael remained standing until she'd taken the chair across from him, then sat down, his back ramrod straight. He might be older, thinner, his mane of hair whiter than the first time she'd seen him, but his presence hadn't diminished in the slightest. He lifted a silvery brow.

"I'm surprised to see you at the mill this early. Is something wrong? Is James all right?"

Her fingers tightened on the carved wooden arms of the chair, and she forced them to relax. Her father-in-law's concern was always for his namesake first. He never called the boy by his preferred nickname, Trey, and never seemed to recognize that he played favorites. He must visualize Trey sitting behind that desk someday, as if her son couldn't possibly dream of anything else. Maybe, if they were lucky, the merger would take the pressure off her son to be what Jimmy hadn't been.

"Both the boys are fine. I've come about something else." She took a steadying breath. "I understand you want me to take charge of Nick O'Neill's visit.''

If she didn't know it was impossible, she'd almost believe wariness flickered in those icy blue eyes. Ridiculous. James Carmichael was always in control. He had nothing to be wary about.

"Where did you hear that?"

She could only hope her cheeks weren't flushing. "I ran into him yesterday, and he mentioned it. Did you know he's renting the Findley house?" And if you did, why didn't you warn me?

"I believe he did mention it when we spoke on the telephone." His expression indicated complete disinterest in where Nick stayed.

She was getting sidetracked, always a dangerous weakness when talking with her father-in-law. She had to stick to the point and make him see this was wrong.

"Is it true? Do you expect me to work closely with him while he's here?"

"Someone from the family should." Her father-in-law always said *"the family"* as if it were in capital letters.

She took a deep breath and tried to remember that she was a grown woman who was allowed to have opinions of her own. "I'd really rather not do it, if you can make some other arrangements." That didn't come out sounding as definite as she'd intended.

"Not?" Her father-in-law frowned at the unfamiliar response. People didn't generally say no to him.

"Perhaps I should have consulted you first, but naturally I assumed you'd be willing to do whatever is needed to make this merger go smoothly. For the sake of your sons, if nothing else."

The comment hit where it hurt. James always managed to find other people's weak points. With her it was her boys. What did he imagine Nick's Achilles' heel to be? She veered away from that thought, unwilling to examine it.

"Of course I want the merger to go well. But I'm not the right person to be working with Nick."

Was it possible he didn't know about, or didn't remember, her association with Nick? He always seemed so isolated from the rest of the town, alone in the mansion on the hill.

Her father-in-law rested thin, elegant hands on the pristine desk blotter. "On the contrary, I believe you're just the right person. After all, you and O'Neill were once...good friends."

So he did know. From Jimmy?

"All the more reason why I shouldn't be involved. You must see that it creates an awkward situation for both of us." She held her breath, willing him to understand.

"For two old friends to work together? It seems the perfect solution."

Her heart sank at the finality in his tone. "But I don't know enough about the mill's operation."

She hoped she didn't sound as desperate as she felt. Maybe she wasn't being entirely rational about this, but she didn't care. "He'll want to know technical details I can't tell him."

He waved a dismissive hand at that argument. "He'll have access to any records and any employees he requires. Your job will be to take him around, introduce him to people, make sure things run smoothly. And, of course, to represent the family."

"But something as important as the merger—won't he expect your personal attention?" She'd never actually argued with her father-in-law, but this hovered dangerously close, and it gave her a queasy sensation in the pit of her stomach.

"What Nick O'Neill expects is of no concern to me." His voice flattened on the words, and his gaze fixed on her icily.

"As the representative of Ex Corp…"

"Exactly." His lips thinned. "You can't imagine I'd tolerate his presence for a moment if it weren't for that."

No, he hadn't forgotten anything about Nick. "If you asked, perhaps Ex Corp would send someone else."

His gesture silenced her. "Impossible. We can't afford the time that would take." He stood up, walked to the window and stared out at the sloping roof of the mill. She could almost sense the intensity of his gaze. She knew, as everyone did, how much the mill meant to him. The mill his father had built, the respect of his workers, the admiration of the town… They were all linked for him.

He turned to face her. The autumn sunlight that poured through the panes wasn't kind. It picked out the shadows under his deep-set eyes, the lines around his mouth. He was always pale, but now his skin looked almost waxen.

"I had hoped you'd do this without argument, Emily. But I can see I'll have to explain."

There wasn't an explanation in the world that would make her want to involve herself with Nick again, but she nodded.

"No one is to know this." He frowned. "Dr. Forsyth tells me that my heart condition is more serious than he first believed. It looks as if I'm facing surgery, and even that may not help."

Her breath caught, a prayer forming in her mind as his words penetrated. She started from her chair, wanting to go to him, but then sank back again. James Carmichael neither expected nor welcomed signs of affection.

"I'm sorry." She swallowed hard, wishing she could comfort him. "I didn't realize. Why didn't you tell me?"

"I didn't think you needed to know."

No, of course not. He'd never relied on anyone else in his life. Her heart filled with a pity she didn't dare express. He wouldn't want that, either.

"But shouldn't all this business about the merger be postponed until you'll well again?"

"No!" He swung to face her. "That's exactly what we can't do. The negotiations had already begun when I found out. You know as well as I do that the mill isn't going to survive without the new business Ex Corp can bring. If they learn of my health problems, the advantage to them would be enormous." He smiled thinly. "I can imagine the rejoicing that would take place if they thought I was in a position of weakness. And that's why no one must know."

"But..."

"No one, Emily. My illness makes it crucial that the merger be completed." The lines in his face deepened. "In a situation like this, one can only trust family. If Jimmy were alive, he'd know how to deal with it. My son had a natural head for business."

Her heart contracted. *Please, Lord, don't let him ever learn the truth about Jimmy. It would hurt him so much.*

"I have to depend on you to take charge of O'Neill. I don't trust anyone else to represent our interests." He didn't sound as if he had much confidence in her ability, either. "Do you understand?"

She understood. The burden of protecting the family was being placed squarely on her, and it wasn't one she could refuse. She nodded slowly.

Her father-in-law leaned on the desk, taking a shallow breath. "Whatever you do, you can't let O'Neill suspect anything is wrong with me." He seemed to be holding himself upright by sheer force of will, and his gaze bored into her. "If he knew, he would be like a shark smelling blood in the water. He'd have no mercy at all."

She wanted to argue that Nick wasn't like that, but she bit back the words. How did she know what Nick was like now? He wasn't the boy he'd been, and she wasn't even sure she liked the man he'd become. He still had that reckless, dangerous edge, and now he had the power to go with it.

But like it or not, they'd be spending a lot of time together in the next few weeks. And she'd have to find a way of dealing with that.

"I'll take care of it," she said firmly. "You can count on me."

The phone rang as Nick started to leave the house. He turned back, picking up the receiver with an impatient movement.

"O'Neill."

"Hey, buddy, how's the prodigal's return going?" Josh Trent sounded considerably more cheerful than Nick felt.

"They haven't exactly welcomed me with open arms." He leaned against the table, Emily's face flickering through his mind. He banished the image and pictured Josh instead, leaning back in his chair in the corner office, the New York skyline dominating the huge windows behind him. "Don't worry. That won't keep me from doing my job. Do you doubt it?"

"Never," Josh said promptly. "But old home-towns can be tricky."

"Mannington wasn't my hometown." Come to think of it, he'd never had anything he'd call a hometown, not the way his father liked to wander. Maybe once he'd dreamed Mannington could be that, but Emily and this town had taught him how wrong that was. "Is that all you called to bug me about?"

"Not exactly." There was a thump as Josh's feet probably hit the floor. "Heard an interesting rumor I thought I'd pass along to you."

Nick's attention sharpened. Josh had an enviable ear for pertinent rumors where business was concerned. "Something about Carmichael Mills?"

"Something about Carmichael himself." Satisfaction crept into Josh's voice. "Nothing concrete, just vague rumblings that maybe this merger is more important to him than he's made it sound."

"Why?" The word snapped as his blood started pumping.

"Don't know." He could almost hear the shrug in Josh's voice. "Just a slight hint of desperation someone picked up. You'll have to ferret it out. Any divorce in the offing? Any family scandals about to break?"

Again he saw Emily's face and was astonished at the anger that surged in response to Josh's careless words.

"Nothing that I can see. But I'll keep my eyes and ears open. Thanks, Josh."

"Anytime, buddy. After all, what's good for Ex Corp is good for all of us, right?"

"Right." Or so the powers that be would have him believe. "I'll be in touch."

Nick stood for a moment with his hand on the receiver. Rumors about Carmichael's motives could be just that. Or they could mean something that would give him an edge in the negotiations.

If there was anything, he'd find it and he'd use it. After what Carmichael had done to his father, he didn't deserve anything else.

His jaw tightened. "Vengeance is mine, saith the Lord," but to his way of thinking, that vengeance wasn't coming along fast enough. If God's will was at work anywhere in this situation, it must be in the fact that he'd been put in a position of power over James Carmichael. And he intended to be sure Carmichael was paid back for every bit of grief he'd caused.

Emily didn't figure into this at all, and it was time he stopped picturing her face and hearing her soft voice whenever the Carmichael name came up. He was here on a mission, and he intended to accomplish it. He wouldn't let any long-buried feelings for Emily get in the way. Remembering how she'd sided with the town against him should be a good antidote.

As he got into the car, he found himself taking an unplanned glance toward her house. He slammed the door. Emily was proving difficult to ignore. Which meant that his resolve to stay as far away from her as possible was the right one. Now he just had to keep it.

The mill hadn't changed in the last fourteen years—that was his first thought when he pulled into the parking lot. Faded red brick of the original structure contrasted with the cement block of the newer section. Biggest building in town—it had always been, and he supposed it still was—lurking over every other structure like some hungry creature. It was a testament to the influence James Carmichael wielded.

Late marigolds bordered the walkway leading to the offices. Nick started up the walk, glancing toward the chain-link gate that lead to the workers' entrance. That was the entrance his father had always used. He'd never, to Nick's certain knowledge, walked in the front door.

Striding quickly, Nick pushed open the glass door, hand on its Carmichael Mills logo, and stepped into the marble-floored hallway. And promptly saw the one person he'd told himself he wanted least to see. A surge of pleasure told him his emotions weren't in sync with his brain.

"Emily." He glanced around the hallway, empty except for the two of them. "Were you waiting for me?"

Her smile seemed the slightest bit forced. "Yes. I wanted to show you the office we've arranged for your use while you're here." She turned, her quick movement ruffling the golden-brown hair that brushed her shoulders. "This way."

He followed her down the hallway, his business instincts aroused. What was behind this development? He'd been sure yesterday that she'd do almost anything to get out of leading him around.

His gaze traveled from the top of her hair, muted under the fluorescent light once they were away from the windows, to the neat pumps that were a far cry from the scuffed sneakers she'd worn the day before. In fact, everything about her seemed designed to be as different as possible from the windblown woman he'd found looking down at him.

Brown and white tweed jacket, neatly tailored brown skirt—this wasn't the Emily he remembered. This was a well-dressed, polite, efficient stranger.

"Are you working at the mill?" He'd assumed the board of directors' position strictly an honorary thing.

Emily's swift pace slackened. He fell into step with her, and she looked up at him.

"Media relations—I'm in charge of media relations and publications." She smiled. "It's only part-time. We don't usually have much need for media relations, but what there is, I do."

"I thought you wanted to be a teacher." He frowned back into the misty past.

She seemed surprised that he remembered. "I was for a while. But when the boys were born I wanted to stay home with them. And after Jimmy's death, it was even more important to be with them."

"So your father-in-law came to the rescue." He hadn't meant the comment to be sarcastic, but it came out sounding that way.

Emily's chin lifted. "I do my job."

Now he'd insulted her. "I didn't mean…"

She stopped, then swung open a door. "I hope this

will do. If there's anything else you need, all you have to do is ask.''

He followed her into the office, but his mind wasn't on the stacks of files or the desktop computer. "All I have to do is ask you?"

She glanced up, her topaz eyes a little surprised, a little defiant. "Yes. Ask me."

"I thought you were going to talk your father-in-law into having someone else be my escort while I'm here."

"Yes, well…"

She hesitated, and he thought he detected a faint flush on her cheeks. It brought on a perverse desire to tease her.

"Well, what? Did you change your mind about spending time with me, Emily?"

The flush deepened, turning her skin to peaches and cream. "I certainly don't mind spending time with you. In a business capacity."

He lifted an eyebrow. "I guess that tells me where I stand."

"I didn't mean it that way."

The flash of anger in her eyes startled him. At fifteen she'd never been angry, just anxious to please. She *had* grown up.

"Sorry." He wasn't—not really. Everything that made her different from the Emily he remembered made what he intended easier. "Look, I just meant that I know when we parted yesterday, you intended to beg off this job. What changed your mind?"

She shrugged, turning away. He put his hand on her arm to turn her attention back to him. Her gaze dropped, startled, to his hand, and he realized this situation made her as uncomfortable as it made him. But he didn't want to let go.

"Come on, Emily. What's going on?"

She looked up at him, wary at first, and then a rueful smile broke through. "Nothing really. It's true I thought someone else would do a better job of this, but my father-in-law wants me to do it."

"And is your aim in life to please him?" Anger roughened his voice, surprising him. Why? Because the girl he'd cared about was now tied, irrevocably, to his enemy?

She studied him for a moment, those golden eyes wide. "No, I wouldn't say that. But he is my children's grandfather, and I'm employed by the mill. I owe him something."

Anger carried him to the phone. "Well, I don't." He picked up the receiver. "What's his extension number?"

"Nick, please." She looked at him with a concern that spun the years back, so that he saw again the girl he'd once loved.

The realization jolted him like a kick to the heart. Whoa, back off. You can't let yourself feel this.

"Sorry, Emily." He lifted an eyebrow. "The extension?"

"Four eleven." She frowned. "Honestly, Nick,

I'm all right with this. I'd rather you didn't say anything to him.''

"Mr. Carmichael, please," he said to the anonymous female voice on the line. "Nick O'Neill speaking."

"I'm sorry, Mr. O'Neill. Mr. Carmichael is gone for the day."

His grip tightened on the receiver. He was primed to have a confrontation with the man now, over anything. "Will you tell him I wish to speak with him as soon as possible?"

"I'm afraid I can't." He thought he detected a note of satisfaction in the woman's tone. "Mr. Carmichael has gone out of town for a few days. It won't be possible for me to reach him until Monday at the earliest. Will that be satisfactory?"

No. "Very well. I'll speak with him then."

He hung up, turned to face Emily. Had she known this already?

"What is it?" Judging from the apprehension in her face, she hadn't.

"Your father-in-law is unreachable until Monday." He realized he still had a death grip on the receiver and deliberately relaxed his muscles. Never let them see you sweat, he reminded himself. Not even Emily. Especially not Emily.

"I'm sorry." She gave him that rueful smile again. "Looks as if you'll have to make do with me in the meantime."

Suddenly he knew what it was about being with

Emily that made him so uncomfortable. It wasn't those flashes of the girl she'd once been, distracting as they were. Being with her brought back memories of the boy he'd been fourteen years ago—angry, unaccepted, always on the outside looking in.

He straightened. He wasn't that boy any longer, and if he had to remind himself of that twenty-four hours a day while he was in this town, he would.

"All right, Emily. You win." He held out his hand. "For the time being, I guess we're going to be partners."

Chapter Four

Emily hesitated for a long moment, feeling as if she were about to leap off the high dive board with no assurance there was water in the pool. Then she put her hand in his.

His grip was warm and strong and altogether too much a reminder of the boy she'd once loved. She pulled her hand away as quickly as possible, hoping that her cheeks hadn't flushed. Crazy to feel anything at the touch of someone who meant nothing to her anymore—someone she'd work with for a few brief weeks and then forget. Unfortunately it had been one thing to agree to this partnership in her father-in-law's presence, and quite another when she was this close, this alone, with Nick O'Neill.

She didn't have a choice, she reminded herself.

"Well." She backed off a step and bumped into the desk. "What would you like to do first?" Preferably something that got them out of this small office. "A tour of the facility?"

Nick's eyebrows arched, and she suspected he knew exactly what she was thinking. Then he nodded.

"That's fine. Give me the grand tour, Emily." He swung the door open. "I'm sure you'll be able to answer all my questions."

That meant he thought she couldn't, that he thought her job at the mill was a piece of make-work created by her father-in-law to give her a paycheck. Her lips tightened. Thank goodness no one knew just how much that paycheck meant to her. She strode quickly through the doorway. She'd show Nick O'Neill just how competent she was.

"Where would you like to start? Fiber processing? Yarn warping?"

For just an instant she thought he was surprised at something, either her willingness to show him around or the fact that she even knew the names of the various departments. Then his eyes narrowed.

"Let's start with the dyeing department."

She met his gaze blankly for a moment, and then she understood. "Isn't that where...?"

"Where my father worked." His tone was even, but a tiny muscle in his jaw twitched, and Emily knew exactly what that meant.

She swallowed, not sure whether she was more dismayed by the fact that she could still read him so well or the realization that this was not just a job to Nick.

She had to say something. She couldn't just ignore his reference to Flynn O'Neill.

"How is your father?"

In anything, his jaw grew tighter. "He died last year."

She stopped, turning to face him, her hand going out to him automatically. "Nick, I'm so sorry. I know how close you were."

For a moment she thought he'd take her hand and respond to her sympathy. Then he turned away. "Is it down that way, or has it moved?"

So her sympathy wasn't welcome. Maybe that wasn't surprising. Any hope she'd had that Nick had forgiven and forgotten died. He was angry, still carrying a grudge over the wrong he thought had been done to his father. Angry with the town, probably still angry with her. That hurt more than she'd expected.

"That department hasn't moved, but we need to stop and get hard hats before we go onto the manufacturing floor." She forced herself to concentrate on the job at hand. "And masks, if you want to go into Dyeing."

He gave a curt nod. "Lead the way."

Once they were equipped, she pushed open the heavy door, settling the mask in place over her nose and mouth. Fabric dyeing wasn't nearly as noisy as the rest of the plant, but the overwhelming odors more than made up for that.

Nick stopped just inside the door, his eyes assessing the huge, high-ceilinged room. What was he thinking? He should be checking out the modernized equipment and the safety gear every worker wore. But she suspected he wasn't seeing that at all. He was picturing his father at work here and probably remembering how that had ended.

People had noticed them, and Emily caught the antagonism in several glances. Just as Nick hadn't forgotten, others hadn't, either.

Nick's dark blue eyes were intense above the mask. "Looks as if people know who I am."

"You know what small towns are like." She tried for a light note. "There are no secrets."

His winged brows lifted. "About anything?"

The several secrets she guarded rested uncomfortably. "Well, I suppose there might be a secret or two somewhere. But surely you didn't expect your arrival to be one of them."

"No." Even under the mask, she could see his jaw tighten. "I guess the return of Flynn O'Neill's son would be news."

She should have anticipated the bitterness in his voice, but it took her by surprise. Her first impulse was to reach out to him, but she stamped it down. He hadn't welcomed her sympathy a moment ago, and he wouldn't welcome it now. In that respect he had more in common with James Carmichael than he'd like.

"I meant that people know about the merger," she said carefully. "This is still a one-industry town.

Everyone has a stake in what happens to the mill. I'm sure they're not thinking about anything else."

He looked at her for a long moment, eyes skeptical. Then he shrugged. "Okay. Let's get on with it."

They went from department to department. Everywhere people greeted her; everywhere Nick was eyed with either wariness or suspicion. If it bothered him, he didn't let it show.

By the time they finally reached the clamor of Shipping and Receiving, she'd begun to relax. This was going to be all right. There had been that bad moment when Nick told her about his father, and people certainly hadn't been welcoming, but they'd gotten through this with a minimum of effort and, better yet, no personal involvement at all.

"Shipping and Receiving." Her gesture took in the yard, busy with trucks coming and going. "Do you want to check out the warehouses at this end?"

He shook his head, as if he'd lost interest once they were away from the section where his father had worked.

"I've seen enough for the first time through. Let's get back to the office."

She nodded. As she turned, her heel caught on the hose that snaked across the concrete. She stumbled, arms flying out for balance.

Nick's arms went around her, strong and steadying, bringing a flood of memories. She pulled herself free, feeling the betraying warmth in her cheeks.

"Are you all right?"

"Yes. Thank you." That didn't sound very gracious, but it was all she could manage. Two unpleasant truths stared her in the face as a result of this little expedition. Nick hadn't forgiven or forgotten what had happened to his father here. And worse, the feelings she'd once had for him still lay under the surface, ready to be triggered by the slightest contact.

Emily was still wrestling with the situation when she arrived at the school to pick up Trey and David. The usual row of car-pool moms lined the walk or leaned against cars, waiting for the final bell to sound. Lorna Moore waved and started toward the curb, her wiry red hair bouncing with every step. Emily got out, smiling, and joined her. Talking to Lorna would give her a welcome respite from the question of Nick's return.

"Hi, Em." Lorna did an exaggerated double take at the sight of Emily's business suit. "Whoa, you look dressed to kill. What's going on?"

Emily shrugged. "Business meeting at the mill." She glanced at her watch. "I was afraid I'd be late."

"So? It wouldn't hurt our kids to wait for us once in a while, would it?"

"I'd like to see the day when Lorna Moore wasn't on time for something." She smiled. "You were born with a clock in your head. Admit it."

Lorna leaned against the fender of Emily's car, raising her face to the afternoon sun. "Actually, I think I was tardy once, sophomore year. Remember when I had that big crush on Coach Fosdyke? I hung around the gym too long and didn't make it to homeroom on time. Ruined my perfect record.''

Lorna sounded sincere, but the sparkle in her green eyes belied the complaint, and Emily grinned. But before she could reply, Lorna checked her watch and looked toward the double doors of the brick elementary school. ''Okay, we have time. Give me the scoop.''

''Scoop?''

''On Nick O'Neill. You don't think I've forgotten, do you?'' Lorna screwed her freckled face into something resembling a look of adoration. ''Dreamy. That's what we called him in high school, or something equally repulsive. So, how's he turned out?''

She should have known she wouldn't get through this day without someone asking that question. Better it was her best friend than someone else.

''If we were fifteen again, we'd still call him dreamy, I guess.''

Lorna lifted an eyebrow. ''And now? What does he look like to a grown-up woman?''

She shrugged, leaning against the fender next to Lorna. She tried not to let the image of Nick's face form in her mind. ''Taller. Older.''

''Come on, give.'' Lorna poked her. ''You might get away with that with some people, but not me. What's he really like?''

''I'm not sure.'' That was the truth. She searched for words. ''Attractive. Very attractive. But he seems almost...I don't know, closed in. As if he's got a defensive wall up, and nobody's going to get past it."

Lorna considered that, head tipped to one side. "Well, I guess he might still be bitter. I mean, he was practically run out of town."

"It wasn't that bad," she protested, knowing in her heart it was true. "Anyway, that was a long time ago."

"You don't forget the hurts you got when you were in your teens." Lorna frowned. "I could list every breakup, every bad grade, every time I was stood up. Couldn't you?"

"I guess." The image of Nick's anguished face wouldn't be banished.

"So, what are you going to do about it?"

"Me?" She turned a startled face toward her friend. "What do you mean?"

Lorna's eyes sparkled. "Well, here he is again. You haven't forgotten. He hasn't forgotten. Maybe you ought to see if the sparks are still there."

"Lorna! I'm not looking for romance—you know that. And certainly not with Nick O'Neill, of all people. He's here on business, remember?"

"Just because he's here on business doesn't mean he can't mix in a little pleasure." Lorna nudged her. "How long has it been since you were out on a date? A year? Maybe it's time you threw a little of that caution to the wind."

"I don't intend throwing any caution to the wind,

thank you very much. And certainly not with Nick O'Neill, of all people.''

Lorna eyed her. ''Why not? What's wrong with him?''

''Nothing.'' She wasn't about to tell Lorna her totally irrational fear that Nick would let his bitterness about his father affect everything he did in Mannington. ''It just wouldn't be suitable, that's all.''

''If you ask me, Emily Carmichael, you're a little too worried about what's suitable and what's not.''

''I didn't...'' The school doors burst open, letting out a deluge of children and saving her from finding an answer. ''Here come the kids. I'll see you later.''

But the subject of Nick O'Neill wasn't exhausted yet, she discovered when she got her own two separated from the herd and into the car.

''Mommy!'' Trey bounced on the back seat. ''Guess what?''

''Seat belt, Trey,'' she reminded. David was already buckling his.

Trey wiggled, impatient, and fastened the seat belt. ''Okay, it's fastened. Guess what?''

''What?'' She glanced at him in the rearview mirror as she started the motor.

''We have a soccer game tomorrow. And this time we're going to win, I just know it.''

''Not unless we get a lot better before then.''

Trey ignored his brother's mournful prediction. ''And it's only three more days until the fair starts, and we get to eat funnel cakes, and go on the rides and see the animals. Coach said if we win the game with the Tigers, he'll buy all of us a candy apple at the fair. So we have to win, we just have to!''

"If we don't get a lot better…" David began again.

"We're better," Trey said firmly, and Emily smiled. It was as if she had her own Eeyore and Tigger in the back seat.

"I know you're improving," she said tactfully. "I think David means that maybe you're not quite champs yet."

"But we are getting better." Trey wiggled. "Maybe Nick will practice with us again today. That would help."

Her heart gave a little lurch at his name. "Now, boys, I don't want you pestering Mr. O'Neill."

Trey looked hurt. "We wouldn't pester. We'd just ask him if he wants to play, that's all."

"No." That came out more sternly than she intended, and she softened it with a smile. "That's not fair, Trey. He might be busy, and he wouldn't want to turn you down."

"But Mom, if we don't ask, how will he know we want him to play?"

Amazing how logical Trey could sound when he wanted something. "No, Trey, I mean it. You can't ask. If he wants to play, I'm sure he'll come out."

"But Mom…"

She gave him her best mom look in the rearview mirror, and he subsided. She could only hope his mind wasn't busy with ways to circumvent her decision.

Nick frowned at the financial report he'd brought home from the office, trying to force himself to concentrate on the rows of figures on his laptop. Unfortunately, Emily's face kept getting between him and the screen.

She'd become quite a woman; he couldn't deny that. He'd assumed that job of hers at the mill had been so much fluff, but he'd been wrong. She knew an amazing amount about textile manufacturing for someone who'd always wanted to be a teacher.

Always? How did he know what Emily had always wanted? He was basing a lot on the knowledge he'd gained in the few months he'd lived in Mannington. A few months was all he'd had before the roof fell in, and at that it had been longer than he and his father had stayed some places. Flynn O'Neill always had been afflicted with wanderlust, always seeing some wonderful new horizon that had to be explored.

He shoved himself away from the computer and walked to the window. He ought to be thinking about work, not reminiscing about the past. Emily had a new life; he had a new life. And speaking of her life, he'd have expected the twins to be pounding on his door by now. He had halfway promised another soccer session.

He lifted the curtain aside, seeing movement, and then grinned. Trey and David were kicking the soccer ball back and forth. They were also staying very carefully on the very back edge of their property line. Emily must have given them orders about staying in their own yard.

Was she worried about disturbing him? Or was she concerned about letting her boys get too close? The very thought gave him a strong desire to go out and play.

Without giving himself time to think about it, he crossed to the French doors and went outside.

The twins spotted him as he crossed the lawn toward them. They stopped, Trey holding the ball, and looked at him with identically hopeful expressions.

"Hi, guys."

"Hi, Nick." Trey spoke quickly, and David gave him a shy smile.

Then they didn't say anything. They just stood, looking from him to the soccer ball.

He had to work to suppress a laugh. Emily's boys listened to her; he had to give her that.

"Practicing?" he asked.

Trey nodded. "We have a game tomorrow after school."

"With the Tigers," David added, the corners of his mouth drawing down.

"Sounds like those Tigers might be pretty tough."

"We're as good as they are." Trey bounced the ball. "Well, almost as good." He paused. "We just need to practice some more."

That was obviously his cue. "Want me to practice with you?"

Trey grinned, tossing him the ball. "If it's not too much trouble."

"If it's not bothering you," David said.

"No, it's not bothering me." Now what had happened to his intention to spend the rest of the day working? Well, he'd be better off after a short break. A man needed a break, didn't he? It had nothing to do with the fact that these were Emily's kids, and that he saw her face every time he looked at them. "Let's start with moving the ball."

They dribbled their way back and forth across the two yards. His feet slid on a patch of wet leaves, and he resolved to get some raking done later. The boys should have a practice area that didn't contain any built in hazards.

Emily's yard wasn't much better, he realized as Trey kicked the ball in a flurry of leaves. He'd have expected her to have a lawn service to take care of little things like that. Someone who'd married into the Carmichael dynasty ought to be able to afford life's little luxuries.

"Get it, David," he shouted.

David went manfully after the ball, but Trey beat him to it. David stopped, breathing hard, and put his hands on his knees.

"It's okay." He patted the boy's shoulder. He had forgotten how little an eight-year-old was. "You'll get it next time."

David nodded, pushed his glasses up and charged after the ball again.

A movement at the back window of Emily's house caught his eye, and he stumbled. Emily was watching them from behind the curtain. Why didn't she come out? Maybe she'd had enough of him for one day.

Somehow the thought gave him a little additional energy. He raced after the boys, shouting encouragement as if he'd been coaching soccer all his life.

"Way to go, David. Steal it! You can do it!"

David charged for the ball in response to his words. Trey, hearing him coming, turned to see where he was, and David ran right into his elbow. There was a thud Nick could hear from several feet away. David sprawled flat on the grass and lay there motionless.

"David!" Nick's heart pounded as he raced toward the child, berating himself. He shouldn't have pushed, he should have been more careful....

"Hey, buddy, are you okay?" He knelt beside the boy, sliding his hand under David's shoulders and lifting him.

David's eyelids fluttered. Before he could speak, Emily swooped down on them, snatching him away from Nick.

"David? David, talk to me, honey. Are you all right?"

Nick heard the panic in her voice and reached out a reassuring hand.

Emily brushed it away, eyes blazing. "What have you done to my son?"

Chapter Five

Emily couldn't mistake the reaction in Nick's eyes at her sharp words—hurt, swiftly masked. Biting her lip, she focused on her son.

"I'm okay, Mommy." David rubbed his forehead, blinking his eyes as if to hold back tears. He pulled away from her. "I'm not a baby."

"Of course not." Nick's voice sounded casual, but his hand gently smoothed the hair away from the red lump above David's eye. "What say we let your mom put some ice on that? That's what sports trainers always do."

David sat up a little straighter. "I guess. If you think so."

Nick grinned at him. "That's what I'd want, if it was my head." He held out his hand to David.

Something inside Emily seemed to melt as her son's small hand tucked confidently into Nick's large one. No matter how hard she tried, she couldn't be both a father and a mother. Sometimes a boy just needed a man, and it looked as if this was one of those times.

"One ice pack, coming up." She led Nick and the boys into the kitchen, trying not to hover. "Trey, get me a plastic bag for the ice, please."

She had to stop overreacting to every bump and bruise. Most of the time she could hide her concern from the boys, but sometimes it just spurted out. When she'd seen David lying motionless on the ground...

Enough. David was fine, and she'd made an idiot of herself. She handed the ice bag to David and looked at Nick. Right now she needed to apologize and then see him on his way.

"Sorry. I'm afraid I overreacted."

"No problem." His deep blue eyes hid his feelings from her. He reached out to settle the ice more firmly on David's head. "Okay now, sport?"

David nodded. His attention riveted on Nick's face as if what he thought was the most important thing in the world. "I'm okay. We'd better go practice some more."

Before she could protest, Nick intercepted her.

"I could use a drink first. Soccer's thirsty work." He settled into the ladder-back chair at her kitchen table as if he belonged there.

Emily's gaze clashed with his, and she suspected he knew exactly what she was thinking. She didn't want her sons looking to him instead of to her. She didn't want him to be a part of their lives. She didn't even want him in her quiet, orderly kitchen, filling it up with his disturbing masculine presence.

But short of being rude in front of the boys, she couldn't do a thing about it. She turned to the refrigerator. "Iced tea or fruit juice?"

He smiled. "Just cold water, please."

"For me, too, Mom," Trey said quickly, and David nodded.

It looked as if her sons had a new hero. She found it disconcerting to see them look at Nick with that adoring expression, because she'd probably once worn one very similar.

She filled the glasses, dropped ice in them and set them on the table. If Nick were reading her glance, he'd know it was telling him to drink his water and go home.

He smiled, then lifted the glass in a silent toast.

Trey put both elbows on the pine tabletop. "We're getting better, aren't we, Nick?"

"Sure thing."

"I bet we'll beat the Tigers tomorrow." Trey wrapped both hands around his glass, his expression speculative. "Our game is at four o'clock in the park, you know."

"Trey." Her tone was warning.

He shrugged, putting on the righteous expression he did so well. "I'm just saying, Mom. That's all. It's okay to just say, isn't it?"

Nick's gaze met her rueful one over her son's head, and his eyes filled with amusement.

"Tell you what, Trey. If I get finished with work by then, maybe I can stop at the game. Okay?"

Trey grinned. "Okay."

David removed the ice bag from his forehead. Thank goodness the lump had gone down. "I can play tomorrow, can't I, Mommy?"

"We'll see. Are your glasses still in one piece?"

Nick picked up the pair David had plopped on the table. "I think so." He straightened the frames a little. "Looks like this guy could use a pair of sports glasses."

"Sports glasses?" She had the sinking feeling this was something she should have known about and hadn't.

"Your optometrist should be able to do them. They won't fly off or break so easily."

"They look dorky," Trey said.

"Hey, I'll have you know I never looked dorky in them."

Trey blinked. "You wore them?"

Nick nodded. "Nothing wrong with using the right equipment for your sport. You think Olympic athletes worry about how they look when they're setting records?"

"Can I, Mom?" David seemed convinced, either by Nick's say-so or the mention of the Olympics.

This was undoubtedly something her insurance

wouldn't cover, but she'd scrape up the money somehow if it meant keeping David a little safer.

"I'll give Dr. Morton a call in the morning."

"All right!" David grinned, and he and Trey exchanged high fives.

She caught Nick's gaze on her and refused to meet it. Was he wondering why she'd hesitated? At moments like this she'd love to have someone in whom she could confide about her financial worries. But to tell anyone would be to betray Jimmy's weakness, and she couldn't do that. Not even Lorna knew, and Nick was certainly the last person in the world she'd tell.

"Well, we've probably kept Nick long enough." She got up from the table.

"But Mom, we wanted to practice some more." Trey's lower lip came out. "The Tigers..."

"Yes, we know all about the Tigers, but I need to get supper started, and I'll bet Nick has work to do."

Her glance demanded his agreement, but he just smiled.

"Actually, I'm caught up. But I am hungry. Why don't all of you go downtown with me for some pizza?"

"Pizza!" Trey shot off his chair. "I love pizza!"

"Especially pepperoni," David added. "Could we have pepperoni?"

"Wouldn't be a pizza without it," Nick said. "Well, Emily?"

"I don't think..." Her mind raced, trying to find an acceptable excuse.

His dark eyebrows arched. "Afraid to be seen with me in public?"

"Certainly not." Not afraid, just reluctant to stir up any more talk. Somehow she knew what Nick would think of that as a reason. "We'd be happy to join you. Dutch treat, of course."

He smiled as if he'd taken her acceptance for granted all along. "We'll see about that."

Nick followed Emily and the boys from the car toward Luigi's Pizzeria, wondering just exactly what she was thinking at this moment. The stiffness about her spine suggested she didn't like the situation but was determined to brave it out.

He wasn't sure why it had seemed so important to push her into this dinner. He could tell himself he wanted to do something to bring smiles to those two little kids, but he knew that wasn't it. Or at least, that wasn't all of it.

Emily had always been so concerned with what everyone thought—her father, the other kids, the whole town. He had a hunch that concern still existed, and it both frustrated and annoyed him. Why did she care so much? And how would the town react to seeing Emily and her kids out with the black sheep who'd come back to disturb its serenity?

The luscious aroma of melting cheese curled through the screen, luring them inside. Nick pushed open the door. The boys bolted for a table by the front window.

Same round tables with their red-and-white-checked tablecloths, same jukebox blinking in amber and green, same worn speckled tile on the floor. Even the prices looked the same, and he couldn't help smiling.

They'd come here after the football games, a whole crowd of kids, raucous and celebrating. And Luigi had given them an extra pie on the house because they'd won.

"What'll it be?" He leaned over the table where Emily was dissuading Trey from pulling half a dozen napkins from the metal holder. "Two large, one pepperoni and one plain?"

"I don't think we can eat all that."

He grinned. "Speak for yourself. I'm ravenous. What do you like to drink with it?"

David slid off his chair. "I'll help order it. I know what Mommy and Trey like."

He could tell by Emily's expression that this was unusual for her shy son, and the thought gave him a surprising amount of pleasure. He put his hand on the boy's shoulder, and the sharp angle fit into his palm.

"Good enough. We'll take care of the ordering."

Luigi himself came to the counter to take their order, his white apron stretched what seemed impossibly far around an expanding middle.

He looked at Nick and beamed. "Nick O'Neill! I heard you were back in town. I told Maria, I'll bet anything Nick comes in for pizza. That boy always loved my pizza.''

"Never found any to match it.'' Ridiculous, to be so happy at the first genuine welcome he'd encountered in Mannington. "So, how are you doing, Luigi? Business good?''

"So-so.'' His pen poised over a pad. "What's for you tonight?''

Nick gave him the order, and David chimed in with requests for colas for himself and Trey and an iced tea for his mother. What, if anything, did Luigi think about him buying pizza for Emily and her boys? Was he remembering old times, too?

They carried the drinks back to the table, with David concentrating hard, obviously determined not to spill a drop. Nick grinned at him when they were safely deposited on the table.

"Good job, David.'' He slid into the chair next to Emily.

Memories assailed him like so many charging tackles. Emily next to him after a game, her golden brown hair brushing his shoulder each time she moved. The way her eyes lit with shy pride when she looked at him. The way it had felt, being a local hero after so many years of drifting from town to town.

Local hero. Something bitter rose in him at the words. Good thing he'd enjoyed that, because it hadn't lasted long. James Carmichael had seen to that, with his determination to get rid of the man he considered a troublemaker. And Emily had gone right along with what the town decided to believe.

"Nick?" Trey's voice was questioning, and he realized the boy must have spoken more than once.

"Sorry, Trey. I was thinking about how good Luigi's pizza is. Did you know that your mom and I used to come here for pizza after football games when we were in high school?"

"All of us did," Emily said quickly, hurt and anger warring in her eyes at his pairing of their names. "Your daddy, too."

Nice work, O'Neill. Let your bitterness spill over onto innocent kids, why don't you?

"That's right." His thoughts raced for a way to make amends. No matter what he felt about Emily or her father-in-law, he couldn't say things that might hurt her kids. "Your dad and I played football together, you know. He loved pepperoni pizza just like you do."

Emily's gaze seemed to measure him for a long moment, as if asking what kind of a man he'd become. He stared back, half ashamed, half defiant.

What do you think, Emily? Whatever I am, this town made me.

The pizza arrived, fragrant and steaming, served by Luigi himself, who hovered over Nick until he took the first bite and pronounced it as good as he remembered. By the time Luigi headed back to his kitchen, beaming, Emily was engrossed in helping the boys get their slices and dissuading Trey from burning his mouth on hot mozzarella.

He watched her with her sons, still feeling a lingering shame over his hasty words. She was so gentle with them—that quality hadn't changed from the girl he remembered. But she had a maturity he hadn't anticipated when he'd thought about seeing her again.

She'd grown up. She wasn't stuck in the past, the way he sometimes felt he was. She'd gone on after he left—gone to college, coped with her father's death, married Jimmy.

Had they been happy together? He suddenly knew that was the question he really wanted to ask. Had Jimmy made her happy enough to forget her first love?

He must have. After all, they'd had their boys to bind them together. Now, every time she looked at them, she must think about Jimmy. Jimmy's image would have pushed his out of her heart a long time ago.

Trey put down a half-eaten slice. "Did you know that the fair is next week, Nick? We're going to go."

"And eat funnel cakes," David added.

"And candy apples."

"Seems to me you two are concentrating on your stomachs a lot." Emily reached across the table to hand David a napkin.

"Growing boys do that." Nick tried to remember what he'd been like at that age and couldn't. He couldn't even remember where he and his dad had lived then.

"Tell me about it." Emily smiled at him. Apparently he was forgiven for his careless comment. "These two both had to have new jeans when school started."

"Mom said she couldn't afford us if we grew any faster," Trey said.

Emily's gaze darted toward him, then away. "I didn't really mean that, Trey. I was just kidding."

"Anyway, Nick's lucky." Trey led the conversation determinedly in the direction he wanted it to go.

"Why am I lucky? Because I don't have to buy new jeans?"

Trey grinned. "No! Because you came to town in time for the fair. You're going, aren't you?"

The fair, with another set of memories from the fall he'd spent in Mannington. Another set of memories that included Emily.

He looked at her and caught the full impact of that anxious, golden-brown stare, as if her thoughts mirrored his. That look seemed to pierce right through the protective armor of his achievements and success, right to the boy who'd never quite fit in. It left him vulnerable, and vulnerable was the last thing he'd intended when he'd returned to Mannington.

"I think I'll probably be too busy for that, Trey," he said quickly. "I've got a lot of work to do before I leave."

This time for good. He needed to keep reminding

himself of that. He'd come here to even the score. Once that was accomplished, he'd leave and he wouldn't be back. And until then, it might be safer to avoid any more situations that brought back memories.

Emily tiptoed across the darkened bedroom. She adjusted the quilt Trey had kicked off, then slipped a book from under David's hand. She'd begun to think they'd never settle. She'd come to their room twice to tell them to get to sleep, and both times they'd wanted to talk about Nick.

She slid soundlessly from the room and paused in the hall, rubbing the throb that had begun in her temples. From the moment she'd heard Nick was coming back to town she'd known this wouldn't be easy. She just hadn't anticipated how difficult it would be.

Hand skimming the worn-smooth railing, she went back downstairs. If she went to bed this early, she'd be guaranteeing herself a restless night's sleep.

Why, Lord? She seemed to be continuing a conversation that had already begun. *Why did Nick come back? And why am I experiencing such confused feelings about him? Is there something You have for me to learn in all this?*

The telephone interrupted her thoughts, and she answered it reluctantly.

"Emily."

Her father-in-law's voice caught her by surprise.

"I thought you were out of town." She sank down in the armchair by the phone, massaging her forehead.

"Out of town? What made you think that?"

"Well…" Then she remembered. "I believe Martha told Nick that you were unavailable until Monday."

"Only to him." His voice was dry. "However, I don't intend to come to the office tomorrow. Will you stop by the house on your way in?"

"Of course." She wanted to ask why, but knew better. If he wanted to discuss whatever it was on the telephone, he'd have said so.

"In the morning, then." He rang off abruptly, as he always did.

Emily sat for a few minutes staring at the phone. She didn't want to see her father-in-law. She also didn't want to see Nick again. But it didn't look as if she had any choice about either of those things.

The Carmichael mansion sat at the very top of Maple Street, surrounded by the lesser homes of Mannington's other wealthy families. The house was a superb example of Italianate style, so they said, but it had always seemed cold to Emily, and she found her steps slowing as she approached the glossy black front door.

Her father-in-law had suggested she and the boys move in with him after Jimmy died. It had been all she could do to soothe his ruffled feathers when she'd refused.

Chapter Six

Emily hurried into her own office, eager for a few moments alone to compose her thoughts before seeing Nick. What was in her father-in-law's mind about this merger and the role Nick played in it? She couldn't begin to guess.

The vague apprehension lingered on the edge of her consciousness as she took care of several routine matters. When she started going through her appointment book for the third time, she took a stern look at herself.

She was procrastinating—that was what she was doing. She was putting off the moment at which she'd have to walk across the hall to Nick's office and face him while James Carmichael's cryptic comments drifted through her mind.

Enough. She wasn't the passive teenager Nick had once known, and she wasn't going to hide from this situation. If she couldn't get the truth about the merger from her father-in-law, she'd get it from Nick. If either one of them had a hidden agenda, she needed to know it, because her boys' futures were at stake.

She stood up, fired with determination, and pulled the door open. And there was Nick, fist raised to knock.

"Sorry." He opened his hand in a small gesture of apology. "I was just coming to see if you were in yet."

"I'm here." She opened the door a little wider, trying to ignore the way her heartbeat accelerated. "Is there something you need? I was about to come and ask."

He moved past her into the office, and once again she had that sense that he was taking over her space. He prowled across the room, seeming in no hurry to get to business. His gaze touched the photograph of Jimmy on the bookshelf, then lingered on the picture of her with the boys that stood at the corner of her desk.

She watched him, uncertain how to go after the reassurance she needed. Nick looked different today. His navy blazer and gray flannels were a far cry from the jeans and sweatshirt he'd worn playing soccer with the twins. In some obscure way the more formal clothing put her at ease, establishing this as a business meeting.

Then he turned toward her. The navy of the jacket deepened the deep blue of his eyes, reminding her of that moment across the restaurant table when something, she wasn't sure what, had sparked between them. Memories, she told herself sternly. Just memories.

"I hope the boys weren't too wound up after you got home last night."

So he'd noticed the effect he had on them.

"It only took two or three demands that they stop talking and get to sleep to settle them." She smiled. "Actually, that's normal. Part of raising twins is that they're always on the same schedule. There's never a time when you're dealing with just one of them."

He leaned against the corner of her desk, focusing on her. "That worries you, doesn't it?"

"Sometimes." She moved so that she could see the photo. How could Nick still read her so easily, after all these years? "I'd like to have more one-on-one time with them, but it never seems to happen. I don't think it bothers Trey, but David...." She let that trail off, not sure she wanted to discuss her boys with him.

"If Jimmy were here, it wouldn't be a problem."

"I guess not." She touched the silver frame of the picture, feeling the cool metal under her fingertips. "Sometimes I think it would be easier to be a single parent if they'd been girls." She smiled. "Not that I'd trade them for an instant."

He shifted, and the movement put him a little closer to her. "I'm not very good with kids, but I'd say you're doing a great job from what I can see."

"Not good with kids?" Her eyebrows lifted. "Then why can't my two stop talking about you?"

"Really?"

That was genuine pleasure in his eyes, and the expression warmed her. For an instant she smiled back, feeling as if the years had somehow slipped away and they were friends again. Then he reached toward the photo and his hand brushed hers.

Warmth traveled along her skin, and her breath caught. She took a step back. She and Nick had too much history between them to ignore, and this wasn't safe.

How had they gotten so far from what she intended to say? She'd better get back to business and keep the personal out of the conversation.

"So how did your first day go? Are you finding the information you need about the company?"

For a moment his gaze lingered on her face. Then he shrugged. "It's early days yet. How soon do you think your father-in-law will be back in town? I really need to discuss some things with him."

James Carmichael wouldn't have any problem lying in this situation, but she didn't intend to do that.

"I think he'll be in the office on Monday." Could he read the evasion in her face? "I'm sure he'll be ready to meet with you then."

"I'm looking forward to it." His jaw tightened, denying the conventional words.

Again she had a sense of intentions being hidden

from her. She struggled to find the words that would make Nick open up.

"This merger with Ex Corp—my father-in-law feels it will mean a lot to us." At least that broached the subject.

"Financially?" His eyebrows lifted, sarcasm in his tone. "I should think the Carmichaels were already pretty well off."

If he could see her bank account he wouldn't think that. But he wasn't ever going to know. No one was. She'd go on pretending until the boys reached college age. Then their trust funds would kick in, and she wouldn't have to worry about their futures.

"I didn't mean that." She tried not to let her personal fears creep into her mind.

"So who are you worried about? This town?"

The raw edge of bitterness in his voice stung. Her heart jolted with the realization. If Nick felt that amount of anger toward the town, how much more anger did he feel toward her?

"This is a one-industry town," she said quietly. "Everyone depends on the mill in one way or another. I guess we'd all like to believe that the merger will bring good changes."

They stood only a few feet apart, but the coolness in his gaze put a gap the size of the Grand Canyon between them. Apprehension coiled inside her. This wasn't the Nick she'd known. This was a stranger.

"Mannington can be sure of that." He smiled, but his eyes were cold. "Things are about to change."

* * *

The reason he felt like a creep, Nick admitted to himself as he left the mill that afternoon, was because he'd acted like one. He yanked the car door open, letting the heat spill out. The weather had been more like July than late September the last few days.

No rain had come along to cancel that soccer game Emily's twins were in. Well, he didn't have to go. He slid into the car. He hadn't promised he'd be there. And Emily certainly would prefer it if he stayed away.

Unasked, the image of her face filled his mind, those golden-brown eyes hurt at his harsh words.

He shouldn't have said anything. No matter how much bitterness he felt toward Carmichael or toward this town, Emily didn't deserve to have it dumped on her. She wasn't the only one who'd let him down.

Now where had that thought come from? He'd better keep reminding himself that Emily didn't figure into this equation at all. All right, she'd dumped him, but he hadn't come back because of that. That had stopped hurting a long time ago. Hadn't it?

He could drive straight home. Tell the boys, the next time he saw them, that he'd been busy with work. That would be the best thing for all of them— to cut off any relationship before it got started.

But he couldn't do it that way. He couldn't just let them down, because he could remember only too well what it felt like.

He must have been ten or so, because it had been peewee football. They'd finally been in one town long enough for him to move up to first string, and his father had promised to come and watch him play.

It wasn't easy to concentrate on the game when half his time was spent scanning the sidelines, looking for the figure that wasn't there. Maybe that was why he hadn't seen the tackle twice his size bearing down on him.

A broken collarbone, that was all. But the assistant coach had to go with him to the emergency room, and they hadn't managed to track his dad down for a couple of hours. He'd been busy, probably with a union meeting or a political rally or a demonstration for one or another of his causes.

No, he wouldn't just ignore the soccer match. He'd stop by, speak to the twins, make his excuses and leave. But he wouldn't just ignore it.

The late-afternoon sun slanted through the oaks in the park, dazzling his eyes as he walked toward the soccer field. The oaks clung stubbornly to their color, but here and there a maple announced that it was fall, whether it felt like it or not.

It looked as if soccer didn't get quite the attention football did—the crowd consisted of a handful of parents in lawn chairs along the sidelines.

He saw Emily first, of course. She'd shed the jacket she'd worn at the office and sat talking with another woman. That mop of unruly red hair must belong to the girl who'd been her best friend in high school. What was her name? Lorna. That was it.

For an instant he contemplated a world in which

you made friends as children and kept them. Emily's world, that was. Not a world he'd ever lived in, or would ever be likely to.

Lorna glanced up, recognized him and nudged Emily. He saw her stiffen and noted that she carefully didn't look his way.

He strolled toward her, nodding to anyone who happened to meet his eyes. They all knew who he was, obviously. If you lived in a town where everyone knew everyone else, a stranger stood out. Especially a stranger who came with the baggage Nick O'Neill did.

"Emily." He paused, then held out his hand to the woman with her. "This has to be Lorna. I'd know that red hair anywhere."

She grinned, not looking a day older than she had in high school.

"It's pretty identifiable, all right. Nice to see you again, Nick."

He thought he picked up a discontented murmur behind him. Someone who didn't agree with Lorna, obviously. He ignored it.

"You have somebody playing in this game?" His eyes searched the crowd of navy-clad players surrounding the coach, picking out Trey and David. Then he saw the one who had to belong to Lorna. "The redhead, of course."

"Poor kid never had a chance." Lorna shook her head. "Redheads on both sides of the family tree. I married Ken Moore, you know."

He vaguely remembered Ken from football, a gangly carrottop whose father worked at the mill.

"So you and Ken stayed here."

She shrugged. "We went away to school, but then Ken got a good offer from the mill, so we came back home." She smiled. "Free baby-sitting, with both sets of parents in town."

He suspected Emily didn't enjoy that kind of free baby-sitting, not with the father-in-law she had. He frowned. Why was he thinking about Emily again? He needed to be making his excuses and getting out of here. Then the crowd around the coach broke up, and the twins and the little redhead ran toward them.

"You came!" Trey reached him first, with David close behind.

"Yes, well, I..." This was the moment to wish them luck and say he couldn't stay.

David leaned against him. "I'm glad you came."

The boy looked up, and Nick could read the apprehension in his eyes. That expression jolted something deep inside him.

"Listen." Nick squatted next to the boys. "You're going to do fine, you hear? Just keep your head in the game, the way we talked about. Think about what you're going to do, not about what might go wrong. Okay?"

Trey nodded, bouncing on the toes of his sneakers. "Okay."

"You'll stay, won't you?" David asked.

"You bet," he heard himself saying. "I wouldn't miss it."

He sank down on the grass near Emily as the whistle blew. The kids ran back to their coach.

"You don't have to stay."

Emily's voice was so soft that probably no one other than he and Lorna heard it. And Lorna was studiously watching the players line up on the field, pretending she wasn't listening.

He glanced up at Emily. The sunlight behind her turned her hair into a golden halo, dazzling him. The shock he'd experienced the first time he saw her after his return shot through him again.

Maybe first loves were harder to forget than he'd thought.

"They wanted me to stay. I don't like to let people down."

He thought she flinched at that—inside, where no one could see. No one, it seemed, but him.

Her mouth firmed, and she sent a warning glance toward the cluster of people behind him.

"It's very good of you. I'm sure the boys appreciate your interest."

The words were as formal as if she greeted him at an afternoon tea, and he had to suppress a smile. She'd had those manners even as a teenager. Maybe if you were the doctor's daughter in a town like Mannington, you were born with them.

The game started then, giving him an excuse to look away. Probably giving Emily the same excuse.

Each time he stole a sideways glance at her, she seemed focused on the players.

David ran toward a loose ball, and her fingers tightened on the arm of the lawn chair until he thought she'd break it off.

"Kick it, David!" he shouted and held his breath.

To his surprise David actually connected with the ball. Emily's fingers relaxed, and he thought he heard a small sigh of relief.

"All right! Way to go, David!" The voice, right behind him, was accompanied by a sharp nudge. "Did you see that?"

He turned. The nudger was a girl, probably fifteen or sixteen, with blond hair in a ponytail and a spattering of freckles across her nose.

"I saw."

She grinned. "Sorry. Guess I got carried away."

"Hi, Mandy." Emily gestured toward him. "This is Mr. O'Neill. Mandy is our baby-sitter."

"Puh-leeze! The boys hate that word!" She leaned forward, elbows on blue-jeaned knees.

"So they tell me. Constantly." Emily talked across him as if he weren't there. "Are you still okay to stay with them tonight?"

The girl nodded, her ponytail bouncing. "Sure thing. I'll go home with you after the game."

Emily glanced at her watch. "I wish I didn't have such an early meeting. It's really going to push me to run back to the house."

"Can I help?" The words came out of his mouth

before he remembered that he wasn't going to become any more involved with Emily and her boys. Still, it seemed ridiculous not to offer when they both knew he was driving practically to her door. "I can give Mandy and the boys a ride home after the game."

Emily looked torn between relief and a strong desire to say no. Then someone in the group behind them gave an audible gasp, as if shocked by the very idea.

Emily's lips tightened. "Thank you, Nick. I appreciate it."

"We won!"

Trey bounced so hard that Nick had to take another look to be sure his seat belt was fastened.

"You sure did." Nick smiled at him in the rearview mirror. "And it was your goal that sealed the win."

Mandy leaned back over the seat to ruffle his hair. "You're a hero, Trey."

"And Coach is going to buy us candy apples at the fair." He leaned back, beaming, as if life could hold no more.

"I'm sure your dentist will appreciate that."

The boys didn't seem to catch that remark, but Mandy smiled at him.

"You've gotta have a candy apple at the fair," she said. "It's practically a law. Did they have the fair when you lived here?"

Since the fair was, as he remembered, a century-old tradition, the innocent question made him grin.

"Believe it or not, they really had the fair and candy apples that long ago."

"Are you going to the fair, Nick?" David had been quiet all the way home, but now he reached forward to press his hands against the seat back. "Are you?"

"I have to work, David, remember?"

"But you could go on the weekend, couldn't you?" Those golden-brown eyes pleaded with him in the mirror. "You'd like it if you went."

"We'll see." He wasn't about to promise anything he couldn't deliver, not to a kid. "If I have time, I might go."

"I'm going on the big Ferris wheel this year," Trey announced.

David shot a look at him. "You're not."

"Yes, I am!"

"Mommy won't let you." David's voice went up.

"Last year she said next year, and now it's next year, so I'm going! If you're scared, you don't have to go. You can ride the little Ferris wheel or the merry-go-round."

The squabble had sprung up so quickly, it took Nick by surprise. Should he be doing something about it?

"I'm not going on baby rides!" David turned on his brother, fists clenched. "I'm not a baby!"

Nick took a breath, but it was Mandy who spoke.

"Knock it off, guys." She sounded bored. "You

want Mr. O'Neill to think you don't know how to behave when somebody's giving you a ride home?''

They subsided, although he caught a couple of furious glances between them when they thought he wasn't looking. Mandy would probably earn her baby-sitting money tonight.

He pulled into his driveway and parked, and everyone scrambled out.

"Okay, guys, let's go get something to eat." Mandy waved to him. "Thanks, Mr. O'Neill."

"Anytime."

The boys, doing a little muttering at each other, started toward their house, with Mandy following. Then suddenly David was running back toward him.

Nick glanced toward the car. Had David forgotten something?

The boy skidded to a halt next to him. "Nick, can I talk to you for a minute? Mandy says it's okay."

"Sure, sport." He sat down on the porch steps. "What's up?"

David sat down next to him. He stared down at the toes of his sneakers, as if he didn't know where to start.

"Is it something about the game?" Nick prompted. "I thought you did a good job, you know."

David sighed. "I guess I did better than last time." He fidgeted, then took a deep breath. "Mandy said Trey was a hero. Coach said that, too."

"I heard that," Nick said gravely. This was obviously important to the kid, but he didn't know why.

"Well, I was wondering..." David swallowed. "Well, do you think I'll ever be a hero?"

The wistful question caught him like a fist to the stomach. A hero. An eight-year-old kid, wanting to be a hero, not sure if he dared dream that.

"I guess that depends on what you mean by a hero." He picked his words more carefully than he ever had in any negotiation. "Sometimes people call someone a hero when they really mean he's good at something. Or even just lucky. You know what I mean?"

David nodded slowly. "I guess." He fixed those brown eyes on Nick's face. "What do you think a hero is, Nick?"

Whoa, he was really getting in over his head. But the boy deserved a straight answer.

"I guess I'd say a hero is someone who does what he figures is right. No matter what other people say, or how big the obstacles are, or how afraid he is."

"Oh." David studied his toes some more. Then he looked up. "You mean, like David in the Bible?"

Nick thought about the boy who'd gone up against the giant armed with nothing more than a slingshot and his confidence in God. He put his hand on David's shoulder.

"I'd say that's a really good example, David."

The boy frowned. "I think I'd be scared to fight a giant."

"I think I would be, too," he admitted. "Maybe even David got scared, when he saw how big that giant was. It's not wrong to be afraid, as long as you still do what's right.''

He held his breath, wondering if he was giving any of the right answers. Wondering if Emily would have his head for talking like this with her son.

Finally David nodded. "Okay." He got up. "Thanks, Nick. 'Night."

He held out his hand gravely, as if they were two men saying goodbye. Nick took it, a lump in his throat the size of a baseball.

"Good night, David."

He watched the small figure trudge back across the lawn and wondered how he'd gotten in so deeply in such a short period of time. And how he was ever going to get out again.

Chapter Seven

"**M**ommy, hurry up!" David and Trey charged through the turnstile at the fairgrounds' entrance, their excitement bubbling so much that Emily expected them to float over the barrier. "Hurry!"

She smiled at Gus Traynor, who'd been manning the admissions booth since she was Trey and David's age. "They can't wait."

He grinned back and slid her change across the wooden counter. "Lot of that going around. Have fun."

"We will." She scooped up the coins and followed the boys through the gate, their excitement spreading to her. She couldn't restrain them, because she remembered only too well what it was like. At their age, this had been like the moment in *The Wizard of Oz* when everything changed to color. What was, for the rest of the year, a few empty acres and a scattering of barns became transformed every September into something magical.

She took a deep breath, inhaling the mingled aromas of sweet cotton candy, pizza and sawdust, to say nothing of the odors wafting from the poultry barn.

Trey and David each grabbed a hand.

"Rides first, Mom. Please?" Trey wheedled, his eyes blazing with excitement.

"For goodness' sake, Trey, give me a chance to take a breath. Don't you want to look around first?"

He shook his head, hair falling in his eyes. "I told Brett I'd meet him at the Ferris wheel, soon as I got here."

Brett Wilbur, a year older than the twins, had a know-it-all attitude Emily didn't like. She looked at David, who studied the ground as if the sawdust might suddenly sprout candy bars. It didn't take a lot of mother's intuition to know something was going on.

"We'll walk toward the rides while we look around." She gave her older son a quelling glance. "No pestering, Trey. I want to enjoy the fair."

How could anyone help but enjoy it? A line of nursery school children wove by, holding hands, their eyes huge with excitement. County fair was like having a taste of Christmas in September.

"Winner gets choice," a barker called. "Everybody's a winner."

By the end of the day, of course, some of the smiles would turn to tears as overtired children protested they couldn't walk another step. And more than one adult would wish he hadn't combined fried oysters and potato pancakes with butter crunch ice cream. But even that was part of the fair.

"Hey, guys! Hi, Emily."

Mandy leaned across the counter of the French fry stand to wave, and the boys rushed toward her.

"Hi, Mandy. Is Mr. Lane letting you run the fryer yet?"

Mandy's eyes sparkled. "I'm working on him. Before fair is over he will, you can count on it."

Fred Lane flicked a fryer basket into sizzling fat with a practiced hand and then gave Mandy a mock-fierce glare over his shoulder.

"That'll be the day. I didn't even let Emily do that, and she was a sight more responsible than you, missy."

Emily laughed. "Don't let him get you down. He always told me the same thing." She grabbed Trey, who was attempting to shinny up the counter. "We'll have some fries later."

"Just be sure you buy them from me," Mandy said.

That was another feeling she remembered—that eagerness to sell something and prove you were worth hiring. Every teenager in town who was willing to work prized a job at the fair. She'd spent three fairs working the French fry stand before graduating to one of the dinner stands. That was harder work, but she'd gotten tips.

A jangle of music sounded as they drew near the carnival attractions, and high-pitched squeals reminded her that she didn't like rides. They were swept briefly into a flood of excited children, then out again.

"When I get big enough, I want to work at the French fry stand," David said.

"Not me." Trey skipped ahead of her, then darted back, dodging an elderly couple holding hands. "I want to work at the basketball throw." He lofted an imaginary free throw. "That'd be fun."

She was about to tell him she didn't think the owner of the basketball toss would pay him to practice free throws when Brett Wilbur sauntered out of the crowd in front of the bigger Ferris wheel. He waved a fistful of ride tickets in Trey's face.

"About time you got here. So, you going or not?"

"Sure I am." Trey dug into his jeans pocket for the money he'd been hoarding the last month. "You coming, David?"

David stuffed his hands in his pockets. "I'd rather go on the bumper cars."

"Bumper cars are for babies," Trey snapped.

Before Emily could speak, someone grasped Trey's shoulder.

"You guys still having this argument?"

One part of her mind wondered how Nick knew what the twins were arguing about, while the other observed that the rumble of that masculine voice caused a regrettable weakness in her knees.

"I'm going on the big Ferris wheel," Trey said. "If David's not chicken, he can come, too."

That bravado surely was for Brett's benefit, but she still didn't like it. "If you can't be polite, Trey, you won't be going on any rides."

Trey opened his mouth, shot her a rebellious look, then closed it again.

"I don't see what all the fuss is about." There seemed to be a smile in Nick's voice. "Trey can go on the Ferris wheel with his friend, and David can go on the bumper cars with me."

"You like the bumper cars?" Trey's glance was filled with suspicion.

"Sure do." Nick steered an imaginary car. "I like rides where you get to do something, not just sit."

Emily hid a smile at Trey's expression. He'd been flaunting going on the Ferris wheel with Brett, and now he'd have to go through with it.

"That's settled then," she said briskly. "Brett and Trey will go on the Ferris wheel while Nick and David ride the bumper cars. And I'll wait on that bench."

Nick shot her a mischievous look. "Don't you want to join us?"

"Mom doesn't like rides," Trey explained. "She says they make her seasick."

"Really?" Nick lifted an eyebrow. "I know one ride she likes."

"What?" Trey and David spoke in unison.

"The merry-go-round."

Nick's blue eyes seemed to deepen as he looked at her. Without volition, memory spun her back to the one fair week Nick had spent in Mannington. Her treacherous mind put them on the merry-go-round, colored lights flashing, organ music playing. She'd protested that the carousel was for children, but Nick hadn't listened. He'd lifted her onto a painted palomino with a bright red bridle, his hands lingering at her waist for a moment before he swung onto the dapple gray next to it. The music, the lights, the motion, Nick's laughing face—it had all been part of falling in love.

"Do you like the merry-go-round, Mommy?" David tugged at her hand. "Do you?"

"Well, I..."

"After we have our rides, we'll take your mom on it," Nick said. "You'll see. She really loves it."

There was a challenge in those blue eyes as they met hers, a challenge she didn't know how to answer.

The gate to the bumper car ride opened and people swarmed through, intent on getting the cars of their choice. Nick grabbed the bright red one David had his eye on and held it while the boy hopped in. He snagged what looked like a replica of a '57 Chevy for himself.

With a grind, a crank and a jerk that snapped Nick's head back, the cars started to move. Grinning, David rammed into him, and the cars clanked as if someone had dropped a bucket of bolts.

"Good one, David." The acrid scent of ozone filled the air.

Exactly how, he wondered, spinning the wheel of the bumper car, his knees almost to his chin, had he gotten himself into this? Trouble was, he knew how. He'd seen the look in David's eyes when his twin challenged him to go on the Ferris wheel. He'd known what was coming and he couldn't stop himself from getting in another foot deeper with Emily's kids.

That conversation he'd had with David the night before flickered through his mind. He'd told the boy a hero was someone who did what was right, no matter the cost. How many times in his life could he say that about himself?

Keep your mind on the job, O'Neill, he chided. Don't get distracted from what you came here to do— not by a woman's soft glance or by the momentary admiration in a kid's eyes.

He swung the wheel to cut off an older kid intent on ramming David's car, sparks showering from the connections over their heads, and wondered how he was going to remain focused.

After the ride, they linked up with Emily and Trey. The boys hadn't forgotten the merry-go-round. They grabbed Emily's hands and dragged her, protesting, to the carousel.

He should walk away. Instead, he found himself climbing aboard the platform. And when he spotted a palomino with a red bridle, he couldn't keep himself from grabbing it.

"This one, guys." He looked a challenge at Emily as he spoke to her kids. "This is the one your mom likes."

Go on, Emily, deny it.

A flush rose in her cheeks, but she reached for the saddle horn, her hand brushing his. Before she could protest, he caught her by the waist and hoisted her onto the glossy painted steed.

He felt the quick catch of her breath and drew his hands away. This was dangerous, too dangerous. Too many memories crowded in on him—memories of that night at the fair, of walking Emily home, linked hands swinging between them, of kissing her in the moonlight just outside the reach of the street lamp.

Remember the other night, he told himself, climbing onto the horse next to hers as the twins swarmed onto the pair in front. When he started getting mushy about his first love, he'd better remind himself of the night it ended. Of the fact that Emily hadn't loved him enough to believe in him.

That was the antidote to the soft memories. He managed a smile for the boys as the music started and the carousel came to life. Hold on to the bitter memories and think about why he'd come back to Mannington.

After the ride the boys took it for granted he'd walk along with them.

Just for a while, he told himself. Then he'd make some excuse and get out. He didn't have any desire to participate in Mannington's annual fall ritual.

Every other person they passed, it seemed, had a word for Emily and her kids. And a sidelong look for him. He should be getting used to it by this time—the wary glances ranged from mildly curious to outright suspicious. Mannington didn't know what to make of the black sheep's return, that was clear.

"There's the grange stand, Mom." Trey tugged at Emily's sleeve. "Are we going to stop for supper? Please? I want a sausage sandwich."

"Alison's there," David pointed out, and Nick saw the little redhead who played on their soccer team. The boy hung on his hand. "You'll eat with us, won't you, Nick?"

Emily's eyes met his over her sons' heads, and she gave him a smile tinged with the same wariness he saw in everyone else.

"You're welcome to join us if you don't have to be somewhere."

Was that what she hoped he'd say? The old recklessness took hold of him.

"Sure, I'd like to have supper with you. The sausage smells great."

Emily looked away from him, staring at the grill as if entranced by the sizzling sausage or the steam rising from bright red and green pepper strips and paper-thin white onion slices.

"I don't usually let the boys eat like this." She wore a faint frown between her brows. "But fair only comes once a year."

"One serving of sausage and peppers won't hurt them. You're a good mother, Emily."

Her startled, unguarded glance told him volumes.

"I try." A smile tugged at her mouth. "The Lord knows how often I pray for wisdom. And patience. Lots of patience."

Her words curled around his heart as he followed her to one of the long tables set up under a green-striped canopy. Emily's faith was a matter-of-fact, everyday facet of her life. How long had it been since he'd thought of God in those terms? Had he ever?

"Hi, guys!" Lorna lifted a glass of lemonade in a salute. "Come join us."

Emily slid onto the chair next to her with what he thought was a relieved look. Relieved not to be eating alone with him and the boys? He suspected that was the case.

"Hi, Nick. You remember my husband, don't you?" Lorna gestured.

Nick half rose to shake hands with Ken Moore. Ken had filled out some since high school, and his carroty hair had darkened. His greeting seemed friendly enough, but he eyed Nick with the same wary look most of the town seemed to wear.

"So, how are you enjoying the fair, Nick?" Lorna's gaze darted, bright and speculative, from Nick to Emily and back again.

"It's about like I remember." He'd certainly been naïve to think he could come back and not be overwhelmed with memories.

"We've got some new things." Ken's tone suggested he took offense at the idea that nothing had changed. "There's the tractor pull, the country-western show..."

"So, what'll it be?" A teenage boy loped up to the table, whipping out a pad and pencil.

"Sausage and peppers all around?" Nick raised his eyebrows and got nods from Emily and the twins.

"For drinks you can have lemonade or lemonade," the boy said. "We ran out of iced tea an hour ago. Sorry, Ms. Carmichael. I know that's what you like."

"Lemonade's fine, Ted." She smiled at the boy, who blushed and loped away again.

Nick cocked an eyebrow at Emily. "An admirer?"

"Goodness, no." She looked startled. "Ted is Mandy's boyfriend."

"That doesn't mean he can't admire an older woman," Lorna said. "You're just such an innocent, you never notice things like that."

"That's ridiculous." That peachy blush rose on Emily's cheeks.

Lorna had it right, he realized. Emily had been married, had two children, but she still possessed that air of innocence she'd had at fifteen.

As if deciding she'd teased Emily enough, Lorna steered the conversation in other channels. Her inexhaustible flow of chatter was aided by her daughter. He noted with some amusement that Alison was a carbon copy of her mother in personality as well as looks.

He caught Ken's eye. "Do they ever let you get a word in edgewise?"

Ken grinned, face relaxing, becoming again the kid he remembered. "Not often," he admitted. "It's okay. I always wanted a daughter just like her mother."

His face tightened again, as if he regretted letting his guard down with Nick. "I guess you think it was pretty small potatoes, settling down here in the old hometown."

"Not at all." Nick picked his words carefully. "I'd say it's probably a pretty decent place to raise a family."

Ken nodded. "That it is." His glance skipped from his wife to his daughter. "And I'd do anything for them."

Nick stared down at the sausage sandwich that had grown suddenly tasteless. Ken worked at the mill. He didn't know what was going to happen once the merger went through. He couldn't guess that the life he'd picked for his family was about to be disrupted.

His jaw clenched. If innocent people got hurt in all this, that was Carmichael's fault, not his. Besides, he could make sure Ken received a good offer to move south to the facility that would replace Carmichael Mills.

"Look at that." Trey nudged him and nodded toward the corner of the food stand. "There's Mandy and her boyfriend."

Mandy, apparently taking a break from her stint at

the French fry stand, stood close to Ted, smiling up at him. The boy slipped a possessive arm around her waist and whispered something that made her laugh and lean against him.

"They're going steady," David announced. "Mandy told me."

Nick put down his sandwich and frowned at Emily. "Isn't she a little young for that?"

"Young?" Emily raised a startled gaze to his. "Mandy's almost sixteen. The same age—" She stopped as if she'd bitten the words off.

But he knew what she was thinking. Mandy was the same age Emily had been when they'd gone together. When he'd told her he loved her. When he'd urged her to go away with him.

The realization was like a kick in the stomach, and he looked again at Ted and Mandy. They're babies, he thought, incredulous. Babies. Like Emily was when I wanted her to go away with me. When I wanted her to marry me.

The truth stared him in the face, and he didn't like looking at it. He'd been blaming Emily, holding on to his anger and sense of betrayal even while he told himself he didn't feel anything for her. And all the while Emily had been absolutely right.

She could tell something was bothering Nick. Emily sent a searching glance at him as they followed the boys toward the rides again. He'd been preoccupied since they finished supper. Maybe he was trying to think of an excuse to leave. Not that he needed one, she assured herself hurriedly. They didn't owe each other anything.

"Can we go on the rides again, Mom?" Trey tugged at her hand. "It's not so late."

She glanced at her watch. "I don't..."

Nick's fingers encircled her wrist, obscuring the watch. "Please?" His eyebrows quirked, and there was an expression in his midnight blue eyes she didn't understand. "Just a little longer."

She hesitated a moment, then nodded. Nick's fingers tightened briefly before he let go.

She had to resist the urge to close her hand over the warm place on her wrist as she watched Nick catch up with the boys.

He leaned over, saying something softly to David. Her small son's gaze met Nick's, held for a long moment. Then he nodded. Nick squeezed his shoulder. Now what, exactly, was that all about?

"Ask your mom," Nick prompted.

"Nick and me are going on the big Ferris wheel." David's hands clenched, but his voice didn't wobble. "Okay, Mommy?"

A whole host of objections flooded Emily's mind. David didn't have to do this; it was okay to be afraid; no one cared. She caught the warning look Nick flashed her and swallowed them.

"That's fine, David. If you really want to."

He nodded, mouth firming. "I want to."

Amazingly, Trey didn't argue that David was being

singled out for something special. He stood beside Emily, watching as David and Nick moved up in the line. She realized he was holding his breath.

Nick and David reached the head of the line, and the next seat swung down toward them. The attendant steadied it. David seemed to hesitate, and Emily held her breath, too.

Then, with a glance at Nick, David scrambled in.

She watched the tall figure settle into the seat next to her son and let out the breath she'd been holding.

"He'll be okay, Mommy."

Trey so seldom called her "Mommy" any longer that she treasured it when it happened. She rested her fingers lightly on his shoulder. "He's scared."

"He'll be okay," Trey said again. "Nick's with him."

She wanted to object to his calm assurance that Nick would make things all right. But she couldn't, because that was exactly what she felt, too.

She saw Nick double-check David's seat belt, then give him a thumbs-up sign. David's answering smile was a bit uncertain, and then the Ferris wheel swung them up.

The first time they swept around, David wore a frozen smile that made her want to stop the ride and pull him off it. She saw Nick's lips moving. He was talking to David, his hand resting casually on her son's shoulder.

The second time around, David was talking to Nick.

The third time around, he actually let go of the bar long enough to wave at them.

She smiled at Trey. "He did it."

Trey nodded, then looked down and kicked at a clump of sawdust with the toe of his sneaker. "I'm sorry. About teasing him before."

She brushed a strand of hair out of his face, her heart swelling with love. "I know. Don't you think you'd better tell him?"

"I will. But he knows, anyway," Trey said matter-of-factly.

That unspoken bond between the twins had the capacity to surprise her at times. "He'd still like to hear it."

The last bad moment came when the Ferris wheel stopped to disgorge passengers, leaving David and Nick at the very top. The seat swayed gently, and she saw Nick's arm move, as if he gestured at the view.

A few minutes later they were getting off. David bounded toward her, a wide grin splitting his face. "It was so cool, Mom! It really was. You could see everything from on top—the mill, even our street."

Giving in to the need to touch him, she tousled his hair. She didn't dare make too much of his conquering the fear, knowing it might hurt his tender pride.

"That's great, David. Did you thank Nick?"

"No thanks necessary," Nick said quickly. "I enjoyed it. Now I think Trey owes me a ride."

She wanted to thank him for helping David, but the words remained unspoken as Nick maneuvered the next few rides so that they were never out of earshot of the boys.

It wasn't until Nick walked them toward the parking lot that the moment finally came. The twins skipped ahead, leaving them alone together under the trees that surrounded the fairgrounds.

"Stop a minute, Nick." She put her hand on his arm to slow him, then couldn't seem to take it away as he swung toward her.

"What?" His voice was soft, questioning.

"I just... I—I wanted to thank you." She seemed to be stammering the words, and the night kept mixing itself with a long-ago evening when they'd stood under the trees and heard the music of the carousel wafting toward them on the night air.

"You don't owe me any thanks. That was between David and me."

A cloud moved across the nearly full moon, casting his face in shadow briefly, then illuminating it.

"You were kind to my son. Can't I say thanks?" The words came out too soft, too breathless, making her sound like the girl she'd once been.

"Still seeing the best in everyone?" The words should have sounded bitter, but they didn't.

"Isn't that better than looking for the worst?"

Nick's arm was still under her hand, and he stood only a breath away.

"Emily, you..."

That began on a note of exasperation, then died away as he caught her arms and drew her toward him.

"Emily," he said again gently, and then his lips found hers.

Warmth flooded her, and barely recognizable feelings tumbled through her. She should stop this—she wanted this to last forever—

Nick let her go abruptly, and the evening air was cold on her lips.

"Good night." It was a barely audible murmur, and then he turned and was gone.

Chapter Eight

Nick nursed a mug of coffee between his hands and stared out at a sunny Sunday morning in Mannington. If he'd been in the city apartment that he treated as little more than a hotel room between jobs for Ex Corp, he wouldn't even have known without a calendar that it was Sunday. He'd have been insulated from the life around him.

But nobody was insulated from his neighbors in a small town like Mannington, except possibly the likes of James Carmichael, in his mansion on the hill. The Sunday newspaper had thudded against Nick's door, followed by the sounds of his next-door neighbors, apparently headed for an early church service.

He glanced at the clock, then discovered he was at the kitchen window from where he could see Emily's house. Ridiculous, wasn't it? But he stood there, half-hidden behind the curtain, until he saw her and the boys start down the walk. The twins wore identical navy pants and white shirts, while Emily had on a flowered dress of some soft fabric that flirted around her legs as she walked.

They were off to Sunday school, obviously. He let the curtain fall. If Emily was bothered by what had passed between them the evening before, she wasn't letting it show.

A kiss, that's all. Just one insignificant kiss between two people who'd been close once upon a time. Nothing to make a fuss about.

So why was his heart thumping uncomfortably at the memory?

Because it shouldn't have happened. He was here with a job to do, and that didn't include getting involved with Emily again. Their childish infatuation had been over a long time ago.

That moment of realization he'd had when he looked at young Mandy and her boyfriend resurfaced, and he shoved it down again. He wouldn't go endlessly over his feelings, trying to figure out what had happened and why. He would ignore the whole thing.

The telephone rang, inadvertently aiding in that task. He picked up the receiver with a sense of relief. "O'Neill here."

"Hey, old buddy." Josh sounded cheerful for this early hour on a Sunday morning.

"Hey, yourself. Why aren't you sleeping in? Or on the golf course?" Nick leaned against the counter.

Josh made a disbelieving sound. "Are you kidding? Ex Corp doesn't recognize a day of rest, remember? Or is small-town life dulling your edge already?''

"Don't you believe it." The words came out with as much assurance as possible. Nick didn't have any illusions that Josh, despite his buddy/buddy attitude, was a friend. At least, he wasn't a friend in the sense that people like Emily and Lorna were friends. If Josh saw a way to push himself an inch higher at Nick's expense, he'd take it. "So, what's up?"

"That's what I called to ask you. Any scoop on the rumor I passed on to you about Carmichael?"

"Nada." Nick frowned. "He's been unavailable since I got here, supposedly away. I should be able to see him tomorrow."

"The sooner, the better. Donaldson would like this rapped up in a hurry."

Keith Donaldson, vice president in charge of acquisitions, always wanted everything wrapped up in a hurry. Before the target of his acquisition looked too closely at the sweet deal Ex Corp was offering and saw the flaws.

In this case Nick's views coincided with Donaldson's. "Don't worry, I'm moving on it. Carmichael will sign on the dotted line."

And soon after that, Ex Corp would announce that it was too cost-inefficient to keep the Mannington mill open. It would be closed, its operations moved south to another mill, and one more of Ex Corp's competitors would be gone.

"Be sure he does." Josh's voice contained a vague note of warning. "You know how Donaldson feels about losing."

Everyone who worked for him knew how Donaldson felt about losing. Make a misstep that cost the corporation, and you'd be gone.

"He doesn't need to worry." Nick made his words crisp. "This one is in the bag."

After he'd hung up he paced back to the window, frowning out at the sunshine. He'd forced himself to sound confident for Josh because that was how you played the game. If Donaldson suspected Nick was tied up in knots right now because of a brown-eyed girl from his past and a pair of cute kids, he'd be abruptly reassigned to another job.

So the thing to do was get on with things as quickly as possible. And that meant seeing Carmichael.

If Carmichael were back in town, he'd probably be at church this morning. Nick frowned. If, that is, the man had ever left. All of this delay could be just a game designed to remind Nick O'Neill that he wasn't worth the great man's time.

There was one way to find out. He turned toward the stairs. Get dressed, go to church and see if Carmichael was there.

Half an hour later he went up the stone steps to the double doors that stood invitingly open, trying to remember how long it had been since he'd gone to Sunday services. Obviously, if he couldn't remember, it had been a long time.

The organ was sounding as he stepped into the rear of the sanctuary, and for a brief instant the carousel music flashed into his mind. He shoved the thought aside, put on a confident smile and took the bulletin an usher held out to him.

He paused at the center aisle. It had been years, but he remembered where James Carmichael always sat—halfway down, on the right side of the aisle. There wasn't a nameplate on the pew, but no one else would claim it.

Carmichael wasn't in church this Sunday morning. There would have been no mistaking that head of pure white hair. But someone else occupied the Carmichael pew.

Emily sat next to the twins. Her golden-brown hair brushed the shoulder of her dress as she bent to whisper to Trey, and David smiled up at her.

Something settled into place in Nick's mind, bringing with it an absolute certainty. Whatever he'd been telling himself, he hadn't come to church this morning to see Carmichael. He'd come because he wanted to see Emily again. Because he needed to set things right with her, once and for all.

Emily heard the rustle of movement as someone slid into the pew behind her, and the briefest sidelong glance showed her who it was. Not that she'd needed to look. She'd have sensed Nick's presence if she'd been blindfolded.

She frowned at Trey, who was nearly bouncing off

the pew in his eagerness to greet Nick. Then she turned, gave Nick the same polite smile she'd have given anyone else who sat behind her and turned her attention to the bulletin.

When she'd read the announcements three times without having them register, she knew she was in trouble. She seemed to feel Nick's gaze on the back of her neck, and his face, indistinct in the moonlight, kept intruding between her and the page.

How had that kiss happened? Was it her fault? All she'd wanted to do was thank him for his kindness to David, and somehow the situation had slid dangerously out of control.

Dangerous—yes, that was exactly the word for it. She shouldn't relive the moment when Nick's lips touched hers, shouldn't let herself remember the overwhelming emotion. Because if she did, she'd begin having ridiculous dreams of something that could never happen.

Nick probably regretted that moment just as much as she did. The last thing he'd want, in the middle of a business deal, would be an emotional complication.

No, it had been a momentary aberration, that was all. The best thing would be to pretend it never happened. She could only hope he wouldn't attempt to apologize or explain, because that would embarrass both of them.

Reverend Hayes entered the pulpit, and with a sense of relief Emily fixed her attention on him.

By the time the benediction had been spoken, Emily knew she owed Reverend Hayes an apology. She'd listened to his no-doubt excellent sermon on the ten lepers, of course she had. Unfortunately she couldn't seem to remember a word he'd said.

The organ postlude rang out, and people began chatting with their neighbors. The twins leaned over the pew back toward Nick as she turned and held out her hand.

"Good morning. Welcome to worship with us."

That was what she always said to a visitor in worship services. But her heart didn't usually pound this way, and a visitor's hand didn't generate this warmth.

Nick greeted the boys, but he didn't let go of her hand. Then his eyes met hers, and her heart gave a little lurch.

"Emily, we have to talk."

"We don't—I mean, we are talking." She was probably blushing for everyone in the sanctuary to see. She pulled her hand away quickly.

His mouth quirked a little at the corners, as if he knew what she was thinking. "Someplace more private."

She had the sense that he intended to do just what she didn't want—bring up last night, apologize, pull the memory of that kiss out between them to look at and be embarrassed about all over again. At all costs, she had to keep him from doing that.

"I can't just now, Nick." She tried for a smile, but it felt stiff on her lips. "I'll see you at the mill tomorrow, I'm sure."

His lips tightened. "This doesn't have anything to do with the mill."

Donna Carter stopped at the edge of the pew just then, giving her a respite from Nick's intense gaze. She spun out the discussion about the fall rummage sale, hoping that when she turned back Nick would be gone.

He wasn't.

"Let's go somewhere and talk." He said it as if the interruption had never happened.

"I have to take the boys home and get them some lunch."

"I'll walk along with you."

Why couldn't he accept the fact that she just didn't want to discuss this? But that never had been Nick's style. He forged straight ahead at any target, no matter what was in his path.

"I don't think…"

"Hi, Emily. Nick." Lorna paused beside them, letting Alison hurry on back the aisle with the twins. "We're going to the Carriage House for brunch. Why don't you join us?" She smiled at Nick. "You, too, Nick."

Emily's fingers tightened on her handbag. The ten-dollar bill it contained wouldn't cover brunch at the Carriage House for her and the twins. Not that she'd go, anyway, if it meant another meal with Nick across the table, reminding her of emotions she didn't want to feel.

"Not today, Lorna. Thanks, but we have to get home."

She slid out of the pew and went quickly back the aisle, hoping Nick would be held up by whatever he had to say to Lorna's invitation.

Outside, she collared the twins, overcoming their protests that they weren't ready to go home and they wanted to go to lunch with Alison.

"Not this time." Her voice was sharp enough to get their attention. "Let's go home and get changed." She tried to think of something that would distract them from the denied treat. "Maybe we can take our sandwiches and go for a hike." That, at least, didn't cost anything.

Trey showed an inclination to continue pouting, but David brightened immediately. "Let's go all the way to the top of Pine Hill, okay, Mom?"

"Yeah, let's." Trey's pout vanished. "We can make peanut butter and banana sandwiches. Come on, David, I'll race you home."

The two of them bolted down the sidewalk. Emily followed, feet rustling through the fallen leaves. It looked as if…

"Peanut butter and banana sandwiches? Will they really take that over brunch at the Carriage House?" Nick fell into step beside her.

She should have known she wouldn't get rid of him that easily. "Isn't it a little silly for you to be walking home with us when you have your car here?"

"I wouldn't have to if you'd let me drive you."

He smiled at her silence. "I thought not. Come on, Emily. Talking with me isn't that bad, is it?"

She swallowed. This appeared to be unavoidable. "If this is about last night…" There wasn't any good way to finish that sentence.

"About when we kissed, you mean?" His sleeve brushed hers as he kept pace with her.

She would not look at him, she wouldn't. But her gaze seemed to find his face without her permission.

He was smiling, a little ruefully. "It shouldn't have happened—is that what you're thinking?"

"Yes." Probably the women he usually dated would find this a laughable conversation. She decided she didn't want to think about the women Nick usually dated.

"That's not how you used to feel, Emily."

His tone was more serious than she expected. She focused on the boys, skipping through the fallen leaves halfway down the block.

"That was a long time ago. We both should know better by now."

"Maybe we should." He shook his head. "There seem to be quite a lot of things I should know better than to do."

She brushed her hand over the wine-colored mums that made a brilliant display along a white picket fence. She wasn't going to ask him what those things were, but she suspected he was going to tell her anyway.

"I realized something last night."

She stole a glance at him and found he was frowning, staring absently down the street toward the boys.

Then he looked at her. "I owe you an apology."

"It was my fault, too."

He looked startled, then amused. "I wasn't apologizing for the kiss, Emily. Strange as it seems, I'm not the least bit sorry about that."

Color flooded her cheeks. "Then what are you apologizing for?"

"For...blaming you." He shook his head. "I finally got it last night, looking at that baby-sitter of yours and her boyfriend."

"Mandy and Ted?" What did they have to do with this?

"They're hardly more than babies."

She had to smile at the astonishment in his tone. "You know, that sounds awfully old-fashioned for Nick O'Neill."

He grinned. "It does, doesn't it? Maybe I'm finally growing up." He stopped and swung around to face her, sobering. "We were just that age when we went together."

She nodded, wishing she could walk away from this and knowing she couldn't. "Just about. You might have been a few months older than Ted."

He made a dismissive motion with one hand. "Not old enough for you to run away with me, Emily. I can't believe I asked you to do that. Or that I blamed you when you didn't."

"We both..." What? We both thought we were in love? She couldn't say that.

"I've held on to my resentment ever since and didn't even realize I was doing it. I'm sorry."

Her heart ached. "It's all right. We were just kids." She struggled to keep her voice steady.

"Luckily you weren't as immature as I was. If you'd gone with me that night, I don't want to think what a disaster that would have been."

Tears prickled, and she held them back by sheer force of will. "So it all turned out for the best, didn't it?"

"Yes, it did." He sounded relieved, she decided. "No regrets, right?"

"Right."

But if she didn't have any regrets, why did her heart feel as if it had just been trampled?

Okay, he'd told her what he wanted to say. Now he should just walk away. Trouble was, he didn't want to.

They'd almost reached Emily's house when the boys came rushing back to them.

"Nick, we have something to tell you." Trey looked as if he was trying to keep from grinning.

"What's that, guys?"

"You forgot your car at the church!"

The twins erupted into laughter, and he smiled with them.

"Yes, I guess I did. I'll have to walk back and get it, unless your mom wants to give me a ride."

"I can't, I'm afraid." Emily gave him the faint, distant smile she'd give a stranger. "My car's out of commission."

"The car broke down." Trey shoved the gate open by swinging on it. "Mom says we can't afford to get it fixed right now."

Emily went scarlet at his words. "Trey, I didn't...that's not what I meant. I just meant we can't get it fixed today. It's Sunday, so the garage isn't open."

From anyone else, he'd have accepted the words at face value. But something about the exchange set alarm bells off in his head. Emily's embarrassment was out of proportion to what had been said. Why was she looking so worried about something as simple as geting her car fixed?

He followed her up the porch steps to the house, wondering. "Do you need a ride to pick up a rental car until yours is fixed?"

"No." Her startled gaze met his, then slid away. "I don't need a rental car. Mannington's a small town. I can do without a car until it's fixed." She opened the door. "Now, if you'll excuse us, we have a date with some peanut butter and banana sandwiches."

He held the screen for her. "I'll wait while you get the boys started. There's something else I want to talk with you about."

He cut off the objections she was about to make by stepping through the door behind her, then giving her a bland smile.

"Fine." She tossed her bag on the sofa with something as close to a flare of temper as he'd seen from her. "Boys, you run up and change while I start your sandwiches."

"But maybe Nick..." David began, and received a firm look that silenced him.

"Go on now."

The twins, with a backward look at him, hurried up the stairs. Emily whisked toward the kitchen. He was alone and not sure why it seemed important to understand what troubled her.

Nick took a deep breath, looking around the large, square room that must be both living room and family room for Emily and the boys, judging by the unfinished puzzle on the drop-leaf table and the television in the corner.

The big old Victorian was in the right part of town—probably a wedding gift from Carmichael, if the truth be known. But it was comfortable, not elegant, with some chintz-covered pieces he remembered from Emily's home when she was a teenager.

It looked to Nick as if nothing had been spent on redecorating for some time. And that didn't fit the Emily he remembered.

Several things fell together in his mind. The way Emily had clutched her bag when Lorna asked them out to lunch. The way she'd reacted when Trey said she couldn't afford to have the car fixed. The troubled look in her eyes when he'd suggested the rental car.

He was standing there staring at her handbag when she walked back into the room.

"What's wrong?" Her eyes went instantly wary, as if she recognized the question in his mind before he'd even formed it himself.

"That's what I wanted to ask you." He felt his way to the question. "This business about getting your car fixed...Emily, what's wrong?"

"Nothing." Her denial was quick, maybe too quick. "Cars break down. It'll go in for service this week."

Was he making too much of this? Some instinct told him he wasn't, that she was hiding something.

"We're old friends, remember? Whatever's wrong, you can tell me."

She went very still. "I don't know what you mean."

"I think you do." The words came slowly as the thought shaped itself in his mind. "I've noticed things since I got back. Jimmy Carmichael's widow and kids should be set for life financially. Instead I find you worrying about spending the money to go out to lunch or get your car fixed."

"It's not that!" The words sounded defiant, but he could see that her hands gripped each other tightly. "I just didn't want to go, that's all."

"Save it for someone who doesn't know you as well as I do." Saying the words, he realized how true they were. He did know Emily, bone-deep. That hadn't changed, no matter what lay between them. "You're broke, aren't you?"

For an instant longer she glared at him. Then she turned away. "*Broke* is such an ugly word." She seemed to make an effort to say it lightly. "We're getting along on my salary, like everyone else does."

His mind whirled, trying to readjust his picture of Emily. "I don't understand. What happened to the money Jimmy left?"

"There was no money." She looked startled, as if she'd never intended to say the words and couldn't believe she'd done it. "Jimmy…Jimmy gambled."

His heart stopped suddenly at the thought of Emily struggling to provide for her boys alone. How could Jimmy have let her down like that? "But doesn't Carmichael help you?"

"No!" She swung toward him with something like panic in her eyes. "He doesn't know! I can't tell him—it would destroy him. He thought the world of Jimmy."

"But if you need help…"

"I get along fine." That momentary flash of panic seemed to have clarified things for her. She reached out, touching his arm lightly. "Nick, don't worry about it. We get along. I don't want Jimmy's father to know. And I don't want the boys to know. Eventually they'll inherit the mill, and everything will be okay. Things are just tight right now, that's all."

She stood looking up at him, and several things

crystallized in Nick's mind. One was that he couldn't tell himself he didn't care about Emily and her kids. And the other was that the revenge he'd set in motion would hurt them in ways he'd never even considered.

Chapter Nine

The rain that spattered against his windshield as Nick arrived at the mill Monday morning accurately reflected his mood. His mind kept returning to one unpalatable fact. If he succeeded in what he'd set out to do, Emily and her children would be hurt.

He sat motionless behind the wheel, staring through gray droplets at the mill looming over him. They weren't his responsibility, some part of him insisted. Besides, Carmichael would provide for them, with or without the mill. He'd come here to see justice done, and if innocents were injured by that, it wasn't his fault.

A nice rationalization, he thought grimly as he stepped out into the cold rain. His father might have said something much like that. Trouble was, Emily and her kids weren't just some abstract, faceless names. They'd begun to trust him. And he was about to betray that trust for a principle they didn't know about and wouldn't understand.

He hurried into the lobby, shaking the moisture from his jacket. The receptionist looked up, eyes appraising as they rested on him.

"Mr. O'Neill, Mr. Carmichael is in his office now. He wants to see you as soon as you get in."

He nodded, appreciating the wording. James Carmichael was a master of the art of power. He'd set the terms and place of their meeting, and he probably intended to keep Nick cooling his heels in the outer office once he got there, just to remind him who was in charge here.

The implicit challenge quickened his pace as he headed for the elevator. He was about to see the man who'd ruined his father's life, and he was long past ready. By the time this meeting was over, they'd both know that Nick had the upper hand in this situation.

When Carmichael's secretary finally opened the door to the inner office, Nick clenched his fist to keep from adjusting his tie. Confidence, nothing but confidence, he told himself. There'd be no betraying little gestures to tell Carmichael he was nervous, and nothing about his expensively tailored suit or business school tie would suggest the boy he'd once been.

He stepped into the office, hearing the door close behind him. The first thing he saw was the bank of high windows overlooking the mill roofs and yard. The second was the man standing at the windows.

Was his memory playing tricks on him? He'd pictured Carmichael as a giant of a man, of almost mythic proportions. Instead he saw an ordinary, elderly man.

Then Carmichael turned to look at him, and he realized the man wasn't ordinary at all. Age had only accentuated his aristocratic quality, and those piercing eyes still had the ability to cut any lesser man down to size.

Nick smiled, rising to the challenge he saw there, and moved forward, extending his hand.

"Mr. Carmichael. I'm relieved to find you back in the office again. I hope there was no problem?"

Carmichael took his hand for the briefest of contacts. "Problem?" His gaze was icy. "Of course not. One of the advantages to being the company president is the ability to take a day off whenever one chooses."

As opposed to lesser mortals like him, Nick supposed.

"I'm afraid Ex Corp doesn't offer that flexibility," he said smoothly. "And if our transactions can't be conducted quickly—" he shrugged "—we move on."

Carmichael gestured toward a chair, then seated himself behind the massive piece of mahogany that proclaimed his status. He smiled, apparently ignoring the implicit threat.

"I trust you're finding everything you need. Of course, you're already familiar with our operation."

"Ex Corp wouldn't send me in without the necessary groundwork."

Carmichael's silver brows lifted. "Actually, I was thinking of the fact that your father was once employed here. Before his unfortunate departure."

For just an instant Nick was blinded by pure rage. He took a breath, then another. Control. He couldn't let the man know how well that shot had found its mark.

He didn't speak until he was sure his voice wouldn't betray the slightest note of anger.

"Ex Corp isn't particularly interested in past history. We're more concerned about the current financial status. I haven't yet received the detailed tax records we requested. Perhaps you would turn them over to me now."

Carmichael made a dismissive motion with his hands, as if such tawdry details were beneath him. "I'll have Emily get them for you. I trust she's being helpful?"

"Yes." He discovered it was possible to talk between clenched teeth if he really tried.

"I thought she would be." Carmichael leaned back in his chair. "After all, you two were once such friends, weren't you?"

Ex Corp would definitely not approve of an executive who knocked over a desk in the middle of a business discussion. Nick managed a nod.

"How nice for both of you that you can combine business with pleasure on this trip."

Who did he think he'd been kidding? When it came to power, the old man knew all the buttons to push.

But it wasn't going to do him any good. He could win all the skirmishes, needle Nick as much as he wanted about Flynn O'Neill and about Emily. But when it came to the bottom line, he was going to lose the war.

Emily stopped inside the mill door, shaking raindrops from her umbrella. In a few minutes she'd see Nick again.

Something quaked inside her. How could she have done that? How could she possibly have revealed to him what she hadn't admitted to anyone in the four years since Jimmy's death?

She hadn't even told Lorna, who'd been her best friend since nursery school, although sometimes she thought Lorna guessed at least part of the truth.

But just like that, after all those years, Nick walked back into her life and saw things no one else did. Emily bit her lip, staring down at the droplets on the glossy tile floor. Was she that transparent where he was concerned?

Well, if so, she'd have to figure out some way of putting up a barrier. Letting Nick see her innermost feelings could only lead to heartache.

She had to talk to him, that was all. She had to assure herself he wouldn't tell, because otherwise she didn't know what she would do. *Please, Lord. Give me the words. I don't know how to handle this.*

Shoving her umbrella into the stand, Emily walked quickly to the receptionist's desk.

"Good morning, Betty. Is Mr. O'Neill in yet, do you know?"

Betty smiled with the air of one in the know. "He came in about half an hour ago and went straight up to Mr. Carmichael's office. They've been together ever since."

Emily could only hope her face didn't mirror her dismay. Nick might convince everyone else that his only concern with James Carmichael was to facilitate the merger. But just as he'd known her secret, she seemed to know his. And she could only pray that he wouldn't allow his feelings toward her father-in-law to lead him into using her as a weapon.

When she reached her office, she left the door standing open. She'd see Nick as soon as he came down from that meeting. As soon as she saw him, she'd...what? If he'd already told, it would be too late.

Please. She clenched her hands together on the desktop. *Please.*

She heard Nick first, his steps quick and angry on the tile floor. She moved to the door, to be met by what seemed waves of fury emanating from him.

"Nick. Do you have a moment?" She almost hated to speak, as if it might invite him to turn that anger against her.

He swung toward her, and for a moment it was as

if he were so far away he didn't recognize her. Then he focused, frowning. "Can it wait?"

"No, I don't think it can." She held the door wide. This could only be made worse by waiting.

His frown deepened, but he stalked into her office. As soon as she'd closed the door, he spun around. "What's so important?"

She could try and lead up to what she wanted to say, but she didn't think that would work—not now. Not when he was obviously so angry.

"You've talked to James."

"Does it show?" He bit off the words, a tiny muscle at his temple twitching.

"Oh, Nick." Her concern for what he might have said was clouded for the moment by the bitterness she saw in his eyes. "Was it that painful to see him after all this time?"

"Painful? No, I wouldn't call it painful. I'd just call it instructive."

"I don't understand." She was feeling her way, trying to find the source of all that anger.

His lips tightened, as if to hold back the words, but then they burst out anyway.

"He actually had the nerve to bring up my father, after everything he did to him. As if..."

She took a step closer, wanting somehow to ease the pain she read in his eyes. *Please, Lord, guide my words. I don't know what to say, and he's hurting so much.*

"Tell me, Nick. Tell me about your father." She held her breath, waiting for an explosion.

It didn't come. Nick stared down at her, his blue eyes dark with pain. Then he shrugged. "There's nothing to tell. You know what happened."

"I don't know what happened after you left Mannington." This wasn't the moment to tell him she'd waited and waited for a letter that had never come. She reached toward him, putting her hand lightly on his sleeve. "Please. Let me understand this."

He stared at her, his eyes unreadable, refusing to let her in. Then something seemed to ease in him, just for a moment. He shook his head. "Has anyone ever been able to say no when you look at them that way?"

She was encouraged enough to smile tentatively. "Plenty of people." *Including you.*

"Not so much to tell." He moved a step away, and her hand fell from his sleeve. "We tried another town. My dad thought he'd do better with the union somewhere else."

"Did he?" She thought she knew the answer from the way he looked.

"Funny thing about that." Nick's fists clenched. "No matter where he went, people seemed to know about him. Everything he tried went sour, until he couldn't get a job at all. And he knew who to blame."

She wanted to protest that her father-in-law wouldn't have pursued him that way, but what good would it do? Nick was too angry to listen, and she wasn't even sure she'd be right.

"What happened to him?" The words came out softly, as if they might hurt him.

"He died a year ago. Hit by a passing driver when he stumbled out into the road late at night. If I'd been able to get him to come and live with me, maybe it wouldn't have happened."

She reached toward him, compelled by the pain in his voice. "You don't know that."

"Maybe not. But I do know he never recovered from being branded a thief. And I know who to blame for that."

His angry gaze dared her to argue.

"Is that why you've come back? Because of what you think James did to your father?"

"I know what he did." He turned away from her, shutting her out. "But the answer to your question is that I'm here on a job. That's all."

She didn't believe it. That couldn't be all, not the way Nick felt.

"If you wanted to hurt my father-in-law…" She had to struggle to keep her voice steady. "If you wanted to hurt him, I gave you the perfect weapon, didn't I?"

He swung toward her, his face disbelieving. "You think I'd use what you told me against him?"

"I don't know." She had to keep reminding herself that he wasn't the boy she'd known. "Would you?"

His mouth twisted. "Strange as it seems, I'm kind

of sensitive on the subject of a boy's relationship with his father." He stalked toward the door. "I wouldn't do anything to destroy your sons' belief in their father, Emily. But that's all I can promise you."

The door slammed behind him.

She sank into the desk chair, as sapped as if she'd just run several miles. All that anger... Didn't Nick realize what it was costing him? Obviously not, or he'd have found a way to deal with it by now. What harm must it be doing to his spiritual life, to be harboring so much bitterness?

Help me, Father. I don't know what to do.

She pressed her hands over her eyes, as if the momentary darkness might help her concentrate. Helping Nick, however much she might want to, could be beyond her ability. They no longer had the kind of relationship that would allow her to intrude so far into his life.

She put her hands down, stared at them clasped on the blotter. Her lack of ability to help Nick was failure enough. But she couldn't fail to protect her sons.

He'd said he'd never do anything to destroy their faith in their father. She wanted to believe that. But given the grudge he held against her father-in-law, how could she be sure he might not blindly strike out with the closest weapon at hand?

She shoved away from the desk. There was probably nothing else she could say to Nick just now that would help. But she could come at the problem from another direction. She could talk to her father-in-law.

She hesitated, staring at the photo of the twins. She didn't want to do this. But if the battle between James and Nick blew up, her children could be the ones who'd suffer.

"Is this really so important you have to speak to me now?" James leaned back in his chair, looking pale. "I was about to leave."

Emily felt a pang of guilt. He wasn't well, and she shouldn't pressure him. But she had to know what was going on, for all their sakes.

"I really need to talk to you today. About the merger. I understand you met with Nick O'Neill this morning."

She watched him, but not the flicker of an eyelash betrayed anything.

"That's correct." His mouth looked suddenly as if he'd tasted something sour. "I could hardly expect to get through this merger without meeting him, so it seemed advisable to get it over with now."

"Did it accomplish what you hoped?" She so seldom questioned her father-in-law about anything that the very act of doing so gave her a queasy sensation in the pit of her stomach. For the boys, she reminded herself.

He shot her a faintly surprised look. "I would say so." He smiled thinly. "He may have a certain importance in Ex Corp's eyes, but in Mannington he's still the same person he once was."

"He's changed." The words came out before she had a chance to think they may be unwise.

Her father-in-law lifted an eyebrow. "You think so? Of course, you knew him far better than I. And you've seen much more of him since he's been back."

She stiffened. "That was your idea, you'll recall. You asked me to shepherd him through the merger process."

"I didn't ask you to have dinner with him at the fair." He leaned forward suddenly. "Or to walk home from church with him."

She was sure she flushed at the memory of what had followed that dinner at the fair. She wasn't going to think about that kiss, not at all, and certainly not when she was in the same room with her father-in-law. Besides, she and Nick had both agreed it was a mistake.

Not exactly, some part of her mind argued. Nick never agreed to that.

Well, he'd agreed that they were right to part, so it amounted to the same thing. And she would not let herself feel that pang around her heart at the thought.

Aware that her father-in-law was watching her, she tried to smile. "Since I'm working with him every day and he's living in the house next door, he's fairly difficult to ignore. I have to be polite when we meet."

"As long as that's all it is."

"Of course it is." She couldn't remember ever speaking to him so sharply. "I'm not fifteen any longer, and I'm well aware of my responsibilities. To the company and to my children.''

He let the silence draw out for a moment, then steepled his fingers, frowning at them. ''That reminds me of something I wanted to mention to you.''

Not anything more about Nick, she hoped.

''Given the surgery my doctor insists upon, I've decided it's time to update my will.''

''That can't be necessary. You're going to be fine.''

He waved away the protest. ''I believe so, but it's still as well to have everything in order. I haven't done anything about it since Jimmy's death.'' The skin around his eyes seemed to draw tighter.

She clasped her hands together in her lap. She'd never thought about her father-in-law's legacy other than to assume that someday his property would go to the boys. He didn't have any other relatives.

''I've given this a lot of thought, Emily.'' His gaze bored into her. ''I'm sure that Jimmy left you and the boys quite comfortably situated, and of course there are the trusts for their educations.''

''Of course,'' she murmured, wanting to ease away from the delicate subject of Jimmy's estate.

''I suppose some people would say I should divide everything among the three of you.''

She looked up, startled. ''That's not necessary.''

''I'm glad you feel that way, because I don't intend to do that.'' His fingers pressed against each other.

"I've weighed this carefully, and I dislike the idea of having my heritage split up. Therefore I've decided to leave my estate solely to my eldest grandson, Trey."

Chapter Ten

Weariness seeped through Emily as she turned into her street at the end of the day. Thank goodness the car had only needed a new battery, which hadn't been a great expense and was easily taken care of. Unfortunately she couldn't say the same for her latest assignment from her father-in-law. Apparently her father-in-law hadn't realized, when he'd casually said she'd pull together the final tax statements for Nick, just how time-consuming that would be. Finance wasn't her strong suit, and probably just about anyone would have done it more quickly.

It hadn't helped that she'd been still in a state of shock at James's unexpected announcement. She bit her lip, frowning absently at the tree-lined street. She'd always assumed, when she'd thought about it at all, that the twins would share equally in whatever their grandfather chose to leave them. This idea of his to leave everything to Trey had shaken her.

If Jimmy were here, maybe he'd have been able to make his father see how unfair that was. But if Jimmy were here, the problem wouldn't have arisen.

She'd tried to talk with James, but he wouldn't listen. It was his estate; he'd leave it as he decided. When she'd persisted, he'd pleaded fatigue, ushering her out of the office so he could rest.

She rubbed at the frown line between her brows. Somehow she had to make James see that this plan of his was as unfair to Trey as it was to David.

At least the boys would be at soccer practice for another half hour. She pulled into the driveway and cut the motor. She had time to change her clothes, start supper and somehow shake off the cloud that seemed to have hung over her since the moment she walked into the mill this morning.

But when she reached the front door, she realized her calculations had been off. The door was unlocked, the boys' backpacks lay on the sofa and the smell of something cooking emanated from the kitchen.

"Trey! David!" She hurried toward the odor. The twins shouldn't have been home this early, and certainly not home alone. And they knew better than to turn the stove on when she wasn't here. "What are you doing? You shouldn't..."

The words died in her throat. Nick, the sleeves of his dress shirt rolled to his elbows, stood at her stove, flipping something with a spatula. David was setting the table, while Trey rooted around in the refrigerator. They stared at her with looks ranging from wary to guilty.

"Well." She dropped her bag on the counter, giving her heartbeat time to return to normal. "What's going on here? Why aren't you boys at soccer practice?"

"Practice was canceled, Mommy." David's glance said he knew they'd taken a few liberties with her standard orders for what to do in that case. "Coach couldn't be there."

She focused on her sons. She'd deal with them first, before she took up the troubling question of what Nick was doing in her kitchen. "And what are you supposed to do if that happens?"

David studied the floral border of the plate he held. "Call you," he said in a small voice.

"But Brett's dad said he'd give us a ride home," Trey said, shutting the refrigerator door. "So we thought we should save you a trip," he added righteously.

"We thought you'd be home."

"But when you weren't we did just what you always told us to do." Trey looked as if he expected a commendation. "We went to a neighbor."

Nick definitely wasn't the neighbor she'd had in mind. She gave him a cautious smile. "I guess that explains why you're here." After the way they'd parted, this was the last thing she'd expected. Why, oh why, couldn't the boys have gone to elderly Mrs. Sanford's house instead?

"Guess it does." Nick's look didn't give anything away. Maybe he was remembering that bitter conversation, too.

"Thank you." She stared at the griddle, on which Nick was cooking French toast. "I appreciate your keeping an eye on the boys, but you certainly didn't need to cook for them. They could have just had a snack until I got home."

He shook his head, a smile finally creeping across his face. "You've forgotten how hungry boys get at that age. These two guys assured me they were starved."

Emily divided a glare between her sons. "You should have ignored them."

"I couldn't do that." He flipped a piece of French toast with an expert hand. "Besides, I knew you'd come home tired and hungry. It didn't seem fair you'd have to start cooking the minute you got in."

Some of her wariness dissolved in the face of his apparent good humor. If he could ignore what had happened earlier, so could she.

"That's what I do every day."

"Not today," he said. He sent her a sidelong glance, lips curving in a slight smile, black hair tumbling onto his forehead as he bent over the stove. "Unless you don't trust my cooking."

"I didn't know you could." Since there didn't

seem to be anything she could do about this situation, short of being rude, she'd have to accept it.

"Every man should know how to cook. That's what I was just telling these guys." He glanced at Trey. "Plate for the toast, please?"

"Right here." Trey held the plate carefully with both hands as Nick forked golden-brown slices onto it. The aroma filled the kitchen, teasingly reminding Emily that she hadn't had any appetite for lunch.

"Smells good." She started for the refrigerator. "I'll just…"

Nick stepped in front of her, blocking her path. His sudden closeness robbed her of breath.

"You'll just sit down and relax." He pulled out a chair. "We men are in charge tonight. You get to sit and be served."

The argument she was about to make slipped away at his teasing glance. "If you insist."

"We do," Trey said, grinning. "We're the chefs, Mom."

She slid into the chair, very aware of Nick's hands holding it, brushing her shoulders as he pushed it in. Stop it, she told herself firmly. Stop thinking about how good it feels to have Nick here.

Trey deposited the steaming plate of French toast on the table, then scurried to help David fill the water glasses. When an ice cube skittered across the floor she made an automatic movement, then subsided at Nick's warning glance. The guys were in charge.

"So every male should know how to cook, hmm? Where did you learn?"

"Here and there. I learned to cook Cajun in New Orleans and the best way to fix shrimp when I worked in South Carolina. The winter I did a job in New England, I mastered chowder."

"Wow!" Trey's eyes widened. "You've been lots of places. We've never been anywhere."

"We went to Washington on the Cub Scout trip," David corrected. "And Mom took us to the beach last summer and to Virginia to see our second cousins."

"Yes, but we never lived anywhere else," Trey said. "Not like Nick."

"There's nothing wrong with living in Mannington." She made her voice firm and tried not to glance toward Nick. He undoubtedly had other ideas about that.

"Is this okay, Nick?" David gestured to the table, and then he and Trey looked up at him. They wore identical expressions that showed how eager they were to please him.

Something gripped her heart, tightening painfully. There again was the gap she could never fill, no matter how she tried. The twins needed a man to look up to, and right now that man was Nick.

It couldn't be. The bittersweet knowledge filled her. Nick, no matter how much the twins liked and admired him, could never fill that gap. Even if everything else that stood between them vanished overnight, she'd still know that sooner or later—probably sooner—he'd go away again.

Nick slid into a chair, telling himself he should go. Emily was home now, and there was really no excuse for him to hang around.

He reached for a piece of French toast, then paused when Trey, next to him, extended his hand.

"We always hold hands while we say the blessing," Trey said.

He took the small hand in his, then turned to his other side. Emily's smile seemed a little strained, but she put her hand in his. He closed his fingers around it in a firm clasp and bowed his head.

"It's your turn, Trey," Emily prompted.

"Thank you, God, for the food we have to eat. And bless Nick. He cooked it. Amen."

He discovered that there was a lump in his throat. Had he ever been mentioned in a boy's prayer before? It seemed doubtful.

When he'd realized Trey and David were at his door an hour ago, his first thought was to tell them to go home. With the black memories raised earlier by their grandfather still in his mind, he didn't want to be around them. But then Trey had explained that their mother wasn't home, and David had looked so bereft, that he'd promptly forgotten all about their grandfather. He'd experienced a protective urge so strong it should have come with a warning label.

So here he was, having supper with Emily and her

twins, when it was probably the worst place in the world for him. He should have stayed away, but how could he when they needed him?

"Mmm, delicious." Trey smiled at him around a mouthful of French toast. "You make the best French toast in the world, Nick."

"Mommy's is good, too," David said loyally. He took a big bite.

Emily smiled. "That's all right. I don't mind giving the French toast crown to Nick."

He realized, suddenly, that the guarded look was gone from her eyes. She accepted him here, in her house, with her children.

Red lights ought to be flashing in front of his eyes. It would be way too easy to get used to this. He should leave.

He kept telling himself that while they ate the food he'd prepared. Then he reminded himself some more while they cleaned up.

When Emily insisted she'd do the dishes it was the perfect time to make his excuses and leave. And he would, just as soon as he finished kicking the soccer ball around with the boys.

They really were improving. He watched them jockey for position as they kicked the ball around an obstacle course he'd improvised. Now why on earth should that give him a greater sense of satisfaction than most of the high-powered business deals he'd been in on lately?

"You do it, Nick." Trey kicked the ball toward him, a challenge in his eyes.

"You think I can't?"

"I bet you can't get to the end without us stealing the ball."

With Emily's revelation about Jimmy's gambling fresh in his mind, his stomach roiled at the innocent phrase. He kicked the ball toward the lawn chair that was the first obstacle.

"I won't bet you, but I'll give it a try."

He almost made it. David nipped in at the last obstacle, neatly swiping the ball away before he could gain control.

"All right! Good one, David. Now you give it a try."

He collapsed on the grass, breathing harder than he ought to from this little bit of exercise. Trey flopped down beside him.

"You're doing a good job, Trey." He leaned back on his elbows. "I'll bet Coach plays you a lot the next game."

Trey nodded, watching his brother. David stumbled over the third lawn chair, lost the ball, then recovered it and tried again.

"David's better, too."

"He sure is."

"But he's not as good as I am at soccer." That could have sounded like bragging, but it didn't. Instead, Trey sounded almost guilty.

"People are good at different things," he said cautiously, not sure what the boy was driving at.

Trey nodded vigorously. "That's what I told him. He's lots better than I am at math."

"What did he say when you told him that?"

Trey stared down at the grass. "He said nobody ever got to be on a team for math. And he'd rather be good at soccer."

He was tempted to say that math might serve them both better in the long run, but he had sense enough to know this conversation wasn't really about math or soccer. "What do you think about it?"

"See, Nick, it's like this." The boy looked up at him, intent, and Nick knew he was about to be entrusted with something important. "Me and David are twins. That's even better than just being brothers. We always did everything together."

Trey stopped, as if he'd just come to a hurdle that was too high to leap.

"So, now that you're getting older, sometimes you want to do different things?"

"I guess." Trey frowned, grappling with the words. "But sometimes maybe we want to do the same things, but one of us is better than the other one. And that makes the other one feel bad. And then the first one—the one that does better—well, he feels bad, too. So he thinks, well, maybe he should, you know, not try so hard."

Once again he was in way over his head with Emily's kids. He recognized a cowardly desire to duck the question, say he had to leave—anything. But the boy was looking at him as if he had all the answers.

"You know, Trey..." Where were the answers to questions like these? He didn't remember having talks like this with his father. He'd just have to wing it. "The way I figure it, everyone's born with some special talents that are just his. Even twins aren't exactly alike that way. I mean, it would be wrong if your mom gave one of you more allowance than the other one. But it's not wrong for one of you to have a talent the other one doesn't."

Trey's forehead wrinkled, but he nodded. "Mommy says God gives everybody special gifts."

He felt uncomfortable heading into theological territory, but he forged ahead. "That's true. So if somebody didn't try to do his best with his special gifts, that would be like saying God didn't know what He was doing."

He was considering each word as if it were part of a legal contract. No, as if it were far more important than a legal contract. How did parents ever figure out the answers to questions like these?

Trey nodded slowly. "So it's okay if one guy is, like, better at one thing than somebody else."

"As long as he doesn't make the mistake of thinking his special gift is more important than anyone else's."

Trey nodded. Then he looked up, and his serious expression dissolved in a smile. "Hey, there's Alison!'' He jumped to his feet and ran toward the girl who had the same red hair as her mother, Lorna.

Nick leaned his elbows on his knees. Apparently the advice corner was closed. Had he said the right thing? Maybe he'd never know.

With Alison's arrival, he had a good excuse to stop. The three kids chased each other around the yard with an excess of energy he could only envy. Now it was time to leave.

But Emily had come out and was relaxing on the porch swing. As if drawn by a magnet, he climbed the steps and sat next to her.

"Don't they ever tire out?"

"If they do, they won't admit it while Alison's here." Emily smiled, shaking her head. "Alison is *very* competitive. She always wants to run fastest, climb the highest—you name it. The boys wouldn't want her to think they can't keep up."

At the moment, Alison was hanging upside down from the limb of the tall maple tree. Her long braids dangled. "Bet you can't do this!"

"Bet I can!" Trey scrambled onto the low branch. "See?"

In a moment the three of them hung there, with David looking a bit green.

"You look like three bats, hanging by your tails," Emily called. "Get down, you're making me dizzy."

Nick watched her lovely face as the children plopped down onto the grass. It was filled with love, pride and something else. Worry, he decided. Worry was planting an unaccustomed frown line between her brows.

"What's wrong, Emily?" The words came out abruptly. "You've been worried about something since you got home."

"No, I'm not." Her gaze met his, startled, then slipped away. She studied the bronze chrysanthemums the setting sun turned to flame. "I'm not worried about a thing."

He put his hand over hers where it lay between them on the slats of the swing. "You know, it's a good thing you didn't decide to become an actress. That was really not convincing."

Her eyes met his, half exasperated, half laughing. "I don't know how you do that."

"Old friends," he said, trying to keep it light. "You can never fool them." His fingers tightened. "Look, is it me? I guess I was pretty rough on you this morning. I didn't mean to be, but…"

"But he upset you." She didn't need to spell out who "he" was. "I'm afraid he upset me, too."

"What did he say to you?" He made an effort to keep the words from sounding harsh. If he came on too strongly, she'd never tell him what was bothering her.

She shrugged, frowning. "Nothing. I—I shouldn't have let it upset me so much. He's an old man. He has a right to be a little eccentric if he wants to be."

Something told him to proceed with care. "Just how eccentric is he being?"

"I shouldn't…"

"Anything you tell me won't go any farther, Emily. We're friends, remember?"

He could see the exact moment when the need to confide in someone overcame her.

"He started talking about revising his will." The words spilled out. "He said…he said he didn't want to split things up. He's decided he's going to leave everything just to Trey, because he's the eldest grandchild."

For an instant he couldn't say a word, because rage choked him. If that wasn't typical of that old tyrant, trying to manipulate a pair of children. And maybe it was a good thing he couldn't speak, because if he said what he really thought, Emily would never trust him with a secret again.

He didn't say anything until he was sure his voice was under control. "I wouldn't worry too much." He stroked the back of her hand soothingly as the porch swing creaked back and forth. "He's probably just talking. Anyway, he's a tough old bird. It'll be years before you have to deal with it. He'll change his will a dozen times over before he's done."

"Do you think so?"

There was so much relief in her eyes that he was glad he hadn't given in to the urge to tell her what he really thought.

"Sure." He patted her hand. "That's just what I think."

Actually, what he thought was that it might be a

very good thing for Emily and her kids when the mill closed. That would end Carmichael's obsession, and in the long run it would set them all free of it. Trouble was, he didn't think Emily would see it that way.

"Hey, everybody!"

Mandy came around the corner of the house, closely followed by Ted. All three kids ran to greet them, the twins tackling Ted's legs like a couple of puppies.

Nick lifted an eyebrow. "Are you running an open house?"

"We do seem to be popular, don't we?" She smiled. "Hi, kids. Come and sit down."

"We can just stay a minute." Mandy plopped down on the porch step, while Ted wrestled on the grass with the twins. "I have to ask you a big favor."

"You want to get out of sitting with the twins?" Emily smiled, as if sure it couldn't be that.

"You know I love the guys." Mandy grinned. "Besides, I need the money. I'm saving up for a new dress for the Harvest Ball."

"I remember."

She was probably talking about the dress Mandy wanted, but that wasn't what leaped into Nick's mind. The words released a flood of memories he hadn't known he had of the Harvest Ball they'd attended together. Emily had worn a pale peach dress, and she'd looked like an angel. He'd thought he was the luckiest guy in the world when she accepted his class ring that night.

"Well, anyway, the dance is Saturday, and we have

a little bit of a problem.'' Mandy approached whatever it was carefully. "You see, some of our chaperons canceled out. So we thought—we hoped— maybe you'd be a chaperon. Please, Emily?''

He could feel Emily's reluctance as if it radiated from her skin. And he knew why. He knew she was remembering just what he was. Their dance, and its bitter aftermath.

He felt her take a breath. "Yes, of course I'll help, if you really need me.''

"Oh, wow, that's great!'' Mandy clasped her hands together. "Thank you so much.''

Emily was carefully not looking at him. "It will be fun,'' she said without much conviction in her voice.

Mandy swung toward him. "What about you, Mr. O'Neill? We need another male chaperon, too. Will you do it?''

The swing stopped moving as Emily seemed to freeze. She wanted him to say no, he could sense it. She expected him to say no. He should say no.

"Sure, Mandy. Sounds great. Count me in.''

Chapter Eleven

"Lorna, I do not need a new dress." Emily stopped on the sidewalk outside the Fashion Flair dress shop, trying to dig in her heels.

"It won't hurt to look." Lorna nudged her toward the door. "Come on, we'll just look."

Trying to stop Lorna from going into a dress shop was like trying to stop a bulldozer from ripping up the earth.

She shook her arm free from Lorna's grip. "All right, you win. I give up. I'll look just for a minute."

Lorna laughed, leading her into the lightly scented atmosphere. "Admit it. You want a new dress for the Harvest Ball."

"I'm not admitting any such thing. I told you, I don't need a new dress."

"Right." Lorna piloted her past the racks of casual

clothes toward the rear of the store. "And what exactly are you planning to wear?"

"Why should I get dressed up at all? This dance is for the high school kids. Who cares what the chaperons wear?" An image flashed through her mind before she could stop it: herself, breathless with excitement at her first big dance, and Nick, handsome in a dark suit.

Lorna shot her a skeptical look. "You know perfectly well Mrs. Adams will be there. She's been wearing that lilac lace dress to every dance she's chaperoned for the last thirty years. You can't let her down by going in slacks."

"I didn't intend to wear slacks. I thought my navy suit…"

"Your navy suit is fine for church. It's not right for a dance." Lorna halted in front of a rack of dresses and smiled at the hovering salesclerk. "We're interested in something dressy."

"We're just looking," Emily said firmly. "All right, not my navy suit. What's wrong with my black dress, then?"

Lorna lifted a scornful eyebrow. "You look ready for a rest cure when you wear black—you know that. Something bright, that's what you need." She ruffled through the rack of dresses.

"I can't afford something new right now."

"Everything's on sale this week," the clerk pointed out helpfully. "Twenty percent off."

They were ganging up on her. She flipped through

the dresses, trying to look as if she didn't like anything. That was the way her whole week had been going. First Mandy, with her insistence on involving her in this ridiculous chaperoning thing. And then Nick.

Why on earth had he said yes? She'd think chaperoning a high school dance would be the last thing he'd want to do on a Saturday night. Especially since...

She slammed the door of her mind on those memories. Maybe she couldn't keep them from coming back in her dreams, but she didn't have to let them in during the day.

Each time she'd mentioned the possibility of getting out of this commitment to Nick, he'd smiled and said he was looking forward to it.

"You've been staring at that black dress way too long, Emily." Lorna said, removing the hanger from her hand. "I told you, no black." She took a second look at Emily's face. "What's wrong?"

"Nothing." Emily glanced toward the clerk, but the woman had moved off to attend to another customer who actually planned on buying something. "Everything. If you think it's been fun, playing intermediary between Nick and my father-in-law while this merger goes through, you're crazy."

Lorna wrinkled her nose. "Guess that would be a problem. How's everything going, anyway?"

"Okay, I guess." She wished she had a better handle on the legal jargon Nick tossed around so easily.

She'd had the feeling all week that the merger had taken on a life of its own, spinning out of control. "The preliminary papers have been signed. Now we have to get through the transition with the rest of Ex Corp's team next week. I just wish James would—"

She stopped, remembering that she wasn't free to confide in anyone, not even Lorna, about her father-in-law's illness.

"Would what?"

"Nothing." She pulled a lavender suit from the rack. "What do you think of this?"

"I think you'd look as if you were competing with Mrs. Adams." Lorna shoved the suit back. "Come on, get serious. You have to find a dress that will knock Nick's eyes out."

"I'm not interested in knocking Nick's eyes out." She tried for a dignified tone.

Lorna grinned. "Sure you are. The man is drop-dead gorgeous. You have to at least look like you belong together."

"We don't belong together." The denial came out quickly.

"You know what I mean." Lorna frowned at an aqua knit. "You can't be more casual than he is." Then she turned the frown on Emily. "Or are you really thinking that you do belong together?"

"Of course not!"

Lorna blinked at the vehemence in her voice. "You don't have to bite my head off. I mean, it wouldn't be such a bad thing, would it?"

"Bad?" Her voice rose, and she controlled it. "I can't get involved with Nick O'Neill!"

"Seems to me you already are sort of involved. I mean, you're certainly seeing a lot of him. And the kids adore him." She grinned. "Even Alison, and she's hard to please."

"That's just business." Emily tried not to think about Nick flipping French toast in her kitchen or kissing her under the trees at the fairgrounds.

"I always did think you two looked great together." Lorna's face lit with mischief.

She rolled her eyes. "Please. We're not in high school anymore."

"That doesn't mean you can't enjoy being with him. Or is this because of that old stuff about his father?"

Nick didn't consider it old stuff, and the insight she'd had into the depth of his bitterness still shook her. "It's not about that—not for me. But you know how people talk."

"Let them talk," Lorna said. "For crying out loud, Emily, you have to do what your heart tells you once in a while." She yanked a dress from the rack. "There!" Her voice filled with satisfaction. "This is the perfect dress."

Emily stared at the peach silk, then reached out to let it ripple through her fingers. If she did what her heart told her, she'd buy it, even if she had to go without lunches for a month. If she did what her heart told her about Nick, just where would that lead her?

* * *

Nick stared at himself in the mirror and adjusted his tie. He frowned at it. Too dark? Maybe so. He pulled it off with an abrupt motion and snatched another one from the tie rack.

Better, he thought, tying it, then smoothing it down. Now, just why did he care what tie he wore to this ridiculous dance? And how had he let himself get talked into it, anyway?

Not that Mandy had done much talking. One thought of the night he and Emily had danced at the Harvest Ball, and he'd signed himself up. He'd tell himself he regretted it, but the trouble was he didn't. Sooner or later all this would come crashing in on him, but at least he'd have had this one evening with Emily.

The telephone rang as he headed for the door, and he snatched it up with an impatient hand. "O'Neill."

"About time I caught up with you." Josh didn't sound quite as jovial as usual. "I thought you were going to call in today."

"Sorry." He bit off the word. "I've been busy."

"That's what Ex Corp expects, isn't it?" There was a slight warning in the words. "That you're busy and producing results."

It didn't take a genius to figure out the pressure was on. "Everything's moving about the way we expected. The preliminary papers are signed. Doesn't Donaldson trust me?"

Josh gave what might have been a laugh, but it didn't sound amused. "Donaldson doesn't trust anyone. You should know that by now. Somehow he's gotten the idea that you're dragging your feet on this one.''

"That's ridiculous." His fingers tightened on the receiver. Was it? Or was Donaldson right for once? "This kind of job takes time. You can't rush people in a small town like this one, especially not in family-owned companies."

"Tell that to Donaldson."

"If necessary, I will."

"Okay, okay, you don't need to jump through the phone at me. Just thought I'd drop a little word of warning, that's all. The man's getting restless."

"He needn't. Everything is on track, and your team will be here next week to do the final transition. If Donaldson doubts it, tell him I said so."

"Sure, I will." Josh sounded placating. "Listen, I know the merger means as much to you as it does to us."

In a weak moment he'd confided in Josh about his father. He'd been regretting it ever since.

"This is business." He kept his voice crisp. "I'm keeping my personal life out of it."

He hung up, wondering if he could really say that about himself anymore. For years he'd driven straight toward success, straight toward a goal of proving that everyone who'd looked down on him was wrong. The goal had taken every ounce of energy, every minute of time. He'd kept his eyes fixed on it, and if life had something else to offer, he hadn't missed it.

Until he came back to Mannington. He adjusted his tie again, knowing full well it didn't need adjusting. Being here had churned up things inside him that were better ignored. This town had an effect on him. This town, and Emily.

"That town..." His father's voice seemed to echo in his mind, from somewhere in the past. *"That town, those people, they hated us."*

He could almost feel his father's heavy hand on his shoulder, could almost smell the scent of failure.

"People like that use people like us. Don't you forget, Nick. They use people like us and then they throw us away."

His mouth tightened. His father had been drinking at the time; he remembered that if he didn't remember anything else. But that didn't mean what he said wasn't true. And maybe he'd better concentrate on business and forget everything else.

His militant state of mind lasted while he drove around the block to the front of Emily's house, while he walked to the door and rang the bell.

Trey and David pulled the door open, four hands grasping the knob, both boys grinning. Mrs. Wilson, an elderly neighbor, stood in the kitchen doorway and gave Nick a wave. She was obviously there to baby-sit, and Nick reminded himself to find some diplomatic way to pay for her services.

"Hi, Nick. Mom's ready to go," the boys chorused.

He looked past the twins into the room. Emily was

coming down the stairs. The overhead light shone on her golden-brown hair, and the dress she wore was the color of peaches.

It was as if he'd taken a surprise punch in the stomach. All of a sudden he was sixteen again, his breath taken away by the fact that he was going to the dance with the girl he loved.

Nick hadn't said a word since they left the house. Emily stole a sideways glance at him across the front seat of the car.

His hands rested easily on the steering wheel, as if he hadn't a care in the world. But he kept his gaze on the road as if he were alone in the car. Was he having regrets at agreeing to do this?

Well, she'd given him plenty of opportunities to cancel out, and he hadn't taken them. So it was his own fault, and if he didn't want to talk, neither did she.

Emily stared resolutely out at the dark street. Autumn fog settled into the valley. It drifted across the road and formed golden halos around the street lamps. Once on a night like this, they'd started for the Harvest Ball together, and she'd been the happiest she'd ever been in her life.

But she wasn't fifteen any longer, and she didn't have fanciful dreams of what her life would be. A dance was just a dance, nothing magical about it. They'd go; they'd watch the kids and drink fruit punch. Then Nick would drop her at her door and that would be the end of it.

That firm resolution lasted until the moment they walked into the high school gym, already crowded with teenagers. Being fashionably late had never caught on in Mannington. A local band played with more enthusiasm than expertise, but no one seemed to care.

"Hasn't changed much, has it?" Nick paused beside her, his hand clasping her elbow, and she had to remind herself what year it was.

"I guess there's not all that much you can do differently with a harvest theme." The predictable corn stalks were piled in the corners, and paper-cut autumn leaves dangled from the ceiling. "Do you remember the fuss over that glass ball?"

"Do I ever." Nick smiled, and for the first time she thought he looked relaxed. A harvest moon hung from the mirrored ball Nick's class had bought over the objections of the class advisor, who'd thought they should buy something educational. "I didn't think Mrs. Adams would ever forgive us."

"She hasn't." Emily smiled up at him. "She'll probably mention it when she sees you."

"You don't mean to say she's still chaperoning dances—the woman must be a hundred and two by now."

A giggle escaped her. "That's probably what the kids think about us."

"They can't possibly." His eyes warmed as he smiled at her. "You don't look a day over fifteen."

She could feel the warmth in her cheeks. It was too much to hope Nick didn't see the effect. "Just wait. By the time this night is over we'll feel every year. Spending the evening with a crowd of teenagers does that."

"Here you are, sir." A gangly boy she didn't immediately recognize slid to a stop next to Nick and held out a yellow mum. "The chaperons all get flowers. There's punch on the table, and if you get tired, we've put some chairs over by the door to the boys' locker room."

She choked back a laugh at the expression on Nick's face.

"Thanks," he said evenly. "If we get tired, we'll take advantage of that. But I think we'll let the lady wear the flower."

The boy blushed. "That's what I meant... I mean, I thought you'd want to pin it on." He looked from Nick to Emily, and his blush deepened. "Have a good time." He made a fast escape.

"You're right. They do think we're a hundred and two." Nick held out the flower, looking at the neckline of her dress.

"I'll just carry it," she said quickly. "The pin might snag the silk."

He put it in her hand, his fingers brushing her wrist lightly. Warmth radiated from his touch, generating a flood of memories, and she drew back quickly, pulse pounding.

He stood looking down at her for a moment, eyes questioning under those dark brows. Then he held out his hand. "I know how to show them we're not as old as all that. Let's dance."

Sheer panic ricocheted through her at the thought of being in Nick's arms. That was the one thing she couldn't do, not if she wanted to keep the memories at bay.

"Chaperons don't dance," she said, trying to sound horrified at the thought. "Mrs. Adams would have us run out of town."

As soon as the words were out, she wanted them back. A muscle tightened infinitesimally in Nick's jaw, but his expression didn't change. "I've already done that, thanks." He took her arm. "Maybe we'd better find the other chaperons and check in."

Pain wrapped around her heart. This was an impossible situation. The whole evening was an emotional minefield, ready to explode at the slightest wrong word or touch. She should have gotten out of this if she'd had to sprain an ankle to do it.

Mrs. Adams presided at the punch table, casting an experienced gaze across the gym as she ladled bright pink liquid into paper cups. She turned a firm expression on Nick and Emily. Her square, ruddy face looked just the same as it had for the last twenty years.

"I expected you people here earlier to receive your assignments."

Emily felt as if she'd turned up late for class without her homework. "I'm sorry, Mrs. Adams. You remember Nick O'Neill, don't you?"

"I never forget a student." She turned a steady look on Nick. "Glad to hear you're succeeding in business. Does that mean you remember some of the calculus you learned from me?"

"Yes, ma'am." He held out his hand, giving her the smile that would charm a statue off its pedestal. "I had the best grounding of anyone in my college class."

While Mrs. Adams interrogated Nick on where he'd gone to college and when he'd received his M.B.A., Emily let her gaze wander across the crowded dance floor. There was Mandy, looking up at Ted with stars in her eyes.

The sight seemed to pierce Emily's heart. She'd looked like that once, danced like that under these same paper decorations and thought she was dancing on clouds.

Nick's hand brushed her arm as he gestured, and her heart lurched. It was probably a very good thing she'd made it clear to Nick she wouldn't be dancing tonight.

The band swung into a slow, romantic ballad, and she stiffened. If he asked her again...

Nick turned to Mrs. Adams and held out his hand

in invitation. "Mrs. Adams, may I have this dance? For old times' sake?"

Mrs. Adams's face flushed the color of an old brick. Then she smiled, took his hand and walked onto the dance floor.

Emily discovered she was gaping and closed her mouth. Of all the sly maneuvers! Nick had just neatly cut the feet from under her every objection. Well, he wasn't going to find it that easy. She'd find some way to avoid dancing with him, because if she didn't... She realized she didn't want to finish that thought.

Mrs. Adams wore the softest smile Emily had ever seen on her when they returned from the dance floor.

"You mentioned our assignments?" Emily said quickly, before the situation could get even further beyond her control.

"Oh, yes." Mrs. Adams resumed her drill sergeant manner. "Keep circulating. Check the rest rooms every fifteen minutes. There's no smoking allowed. And you'd better walk out onto the breezeway a few times, just to make sure no one's out there. The rule is that once they leave the dance, they have to leave school grounds."

"I remember." Unfortunately she also remembered that Nick had stolen a kiss or two on that breezeway.

She raised her eyes for an unguarded moment to find him looking at her, that memory as vivid between them as if it had flashed onto a movie screen. Her heart thumped erratically, and she was fifteen again, feeling Nick's lips on hers.

Mrs. Adams went back to the punch table, and Nick held out his hand to her.

"I think I'd better check the girls' rest room," she said quickly.

Nick lifted an eyebrow, his gaze saying he knew exactly why she wanted to do it at this moment. "I'd ask you to dance, but duty comes first. I'll meet you back here."

She nodded and hurried through the crowd as if someone were chasing her.

The corridor outside the gym was empty. Heels clicking on the tile floor, she crossed to the rest room door and pulled it open.

No one was in the outer lounge, and Mrs. Adams would be relieved to know she didn't smell any smoke. She paused, seeing her own image staring back at her from the mirror.

Her cheeks were flushed, and she pressed both hands to them. She could always use the excuse that it was stuffy in here, but...

"And I told her I was going out with Tim, and you wouldn't believe what she said."

The girl's voice, drifting over the partition, caught off guard. She'd thought the room was empty.

"You can't go out with him." The other young voice sounded determined. "Just think what people will say."

Just think what people will say. She didn't hear the girl's answer, because the words kept vibrating in her mind. *Just think what people will say.* How many times had her father said that to her when she was growing up? He'd constantly impressed upon her the need to behave in a manner befitting his daughter and, good girl that she was, she'd obeyed. Even when it came to Nick.

The rest room walls seemed to be closing in on her. She hurried out, then along the hall to the glass doors leading onto the breezeway. She had to get outside, breathe some cool air, compose herself before she could think about going back inside and facing Nick again.

The cool night air fanned her as she stepped outside, and the closing door shut off the sound of music and laughter from the gym. No teenagers lingered in the shadows, waiting to be chased away.

She took a deep breath, then another. This was silly. Why had she let herself become so panic-stricken? No one cared anymore why she'd done or not done something when she was a teenager. Nick had said she'd been right when she refused to go away with him. Averted a disaster, that was what he'd said. It didn't matter at all that she'd done the right thing for the wrong reason.

She'd go back in and...

The door opened, letting a burst of music out on the cool air, then closed again. She knew, without turning around, that it was Nick.

He stopped behind her. "What are you doing out here?" He put his hands on her arms. "Besides freezing."

Her skin warmed at his touch, and she wanted to lean back against him.

"I just..." The words died as he gently turned her to face him.

"Running away?" His voice was softly mocking, but the glow of the streetlight showed her his face, and it wasn't mocking at all.

She shook her head, not finding any words.

Nick's hand lifted slowly. He touched her cheek, his fingertips gliding across the skin, warming it. Then, inevitably, his lips met hers.

Her arms went around him, drawing him even closer. Home. She'd come home from a long, lonely journey. She was safe in his arms, her heart so full it might burst, and she never wanted to be away from him again.

Nick pressed his cheek to hers. "Emily." Her name came out on a sigh. He drew back a little. "They say you never forget your first love. I guess they're right."

She tried to arrange her lips in a smile, but they didn't seem to cooperate. Was that all it was to him? A reminiscence? A trip down memory lane while he was back in the old hometown?

"We'd better go back inside." That didn't come out as cool and composed as she'd have liked, but he didn't seem to notice.

He nodded. "Mrs. Adams will be after us for setting a bad example."

He held the door open for her, and she went

through it as the music surrounded them again. She might as well not have worried about whether or not she'd dance with Nick tonight, because it hadn't mattered in the least. It hadn't taken a dance to show her that she was falling in love with Nick O'Neill all over again. And Emily knew she was going to get hurt just as she had the last time.

Chapter Twelve

That wave of panic swept over her again as they went back into the crowded room. Love? She couldn't possibly be thinking that, not about Nick. Not when she knew, beyond any possibility of doubt, that it could never be.

Lord, why did You bring him back here again? What am I going to do?

If there was an answer, she didn't hear it.

She clenched her hands, pressing them against the silk of her skirt. If something couldn't be, then you didn't admit it. Not to herself, and certainly not to Nick. He must never know this was anything more to her than it was to him. So she'd keep smiling, keep it light and get through the rest of the evening as best she could.

"Is everything all right, Emily?" Mrs. Adams's wise old eyes seemed to see through her.

She managed a smile. "Of course." She watched Nick, who was working his way through the crowd toward the stage. His broad-shouldered figure made the high school boys look like children, and he cleaved a path with no effort at all.

"Seems to have turned out pretty well." Mrs. Adams apparently had no difficulty in following Emily's train of thought. "After a rocky start."

"Yes." She really didn't want to discuss Nick with Mrs. Adams or anyone else until she'd had a chance to get her own thinking straightened out.

"Funny, his coming back here now." Mrs. Adams wasn't discouraged by the monosyllable, it seemed. "I'd think this is the last place he'd want to be. Unless, of course, he has a special reason...." Her gaze probed Emily, making Emily feel like a worm being eyed by a hungry robin.

"I'd better make my rounds again," she said, and fled.

Nick caught up with her as she reached the edge of the dance floor.

"Just the person I was looking for." He took her hand. "I think this dance is mine, isn't it?"

The loud, fast song blared in her ears. "Not with this music. Maybe Mandy can dance to this stuff, but I can't."

Nick smiled as the number came to an abrupt end. "I predict they'll play something you like."

The band swung into a ballad, and Nick drew her

onto the dance floor. Her breath caught as his arm went around her waist.

Light, remember? Keep it light.

"Now why do I think you set this up?"

A smile tugged at Nick's lips. "It only cost me five bucks." He twirled her around, drawing her a bit closer. "I think it was worth it to dance with the prettiest woman in the room."

"That's not saying a lot, since every other female is either under seventeen or over sixty."

His arm tightened, and suddenly her temple was against his cheek. If he tried, he'd be able to feel her pulse pounding.

"It wouldn't matter if the room were filled with cover models." His voice was soft, and his breath stirred her hair. "You'd still be the prettiest."

Another couple bumped them, and Nick turned her, his movement as protective as if she were made of glass. Everything about the moment, from the smooth wool of his coat to the hard muscle underneath, from the paper leaves to the shimmering glass ball, engraved itself on her heart. She wanted to hold this little piece of time safe, forever.

The rest of the evening passed in the same way. They watched the kids; they talked to the other chaperons. They danced again, and she found she was smiling constantly.

She seemed to be moving in a dream, and yet it was a dream where all the edges were sharp and clear. The sort of dream you never forgot.

When Nick drew the car up in front of the house, she knew it was time for the dream to end. She grasped the door handle.

"You don't have to see me in, Nick."

He didn't answer, just came around the car to open the door and help her out as ceremoniously as if she were a princess alighting from a coach. His fingers tightened on hers.

"I always escort the lady to her door."

"Well, I..." The rest of the objection vanished when he put his arm around her. She had a thoroughly demoralizing need to lean against his strong shoulder.

"Come on, Emily." His voice was low. "It's not as if I never walked you home before."

Keep it light, remember?

"Seems to me we were always about one second ahead of my curfew." She glanced up and saw his smile in the golden glow of the street lamp.

"Your sons don't give you a curfew, do they?"

"No, but the baby-sitter's meter is running."

Just a few more steps, and she could close the door behind her and drop the illusion that this was a casual, meaningless evening between two old friends.

"I'll pay for the extra minutes."

Nick stopped, drawing her to a stop, too. They stood in the shadow of the overgrown lilac bush, between the circle of light cast by the street lamp and that of her porch light.

"I'd better go in." The words came out on a breathless whisper.

"Not yet." Nick ran his fingers through her hair, then along the line of her jaw. Her skin warmed; her breath caught. "We used to stop under the willow tree in your front yard for a good-night kiss. Don't you remember?"

She ought to say no but she couldn't when Nick's touch set every nerve ending tingling. "I remember."

"I didn't want your father to see us kiss." His lips came closer to hers. "Now I don't want your sons to see it."

"Are we going to kiss?" She tried desperately to keep it light.

"Definitely." Amusement threaded Nick's voice.

Then his lips found hers, and everything else vanished in the warmth of his kiss. She nestled closer, feeling the strength of his arms around her as the sidewalk rocked beneath her feet.

An eternity later his lips moved to her cheek, and she felt his breath against her skin. "Emily." He leaned back a little, still holding her, and his gaze met hers. "Spend tomorrow with me. You and the boys."

"I—we have Sunday school and church, then in the evening we have to go to my father-in-law's for dinner...."

"I'll meet you at church, and afterwards we can have the whole afternoon together."

She should say no. She wanted to say yes. Her heart clenched. Nick would leave again soon; that was the way it would be. Surely she could have one lovely afternoon to remember.

She looked up at him and nodded.
"Tomorrow."

The fact that he saw the sun come up was a measure of how much that evening with Emily had disturbed him. Nick stared out the kitchen window at the back of her house. A vagrant breeze took a few more leaves from the maple, sending them groundward in a shower of gold.

Emily, smiling up at him while they danced. Emily, her lips soft under his when they kissed.

That had been a mistake, hadn't it? Trouble was, it didn't feel like a mistake. It felt right. It felt like something that had been delayed far too long, but now was set right at last.

He put down the mug of coffee he'd been nursing. Time to face facts. By the end of this week, his business in Mannington would be finished, and he'd be leaving. He wouldn't see Emily or her kids again.

That was all the more reason to have one last time with them. One day when they could enjoy each other's company without either the past or the future shadowing it.

How much would Emily enjoy his company once the future of Carmichael Mills was known? Probably not much at all. He could tell himself that it would be best for Emily and her kids in the long run to no longer have the mill hanging around their necks like an albatross. He didn't think she was going to see it that way.

One last day, that was all he'd have. So it might as well start as soon as possible. With a spurt of energy he headed for the door. If Emily wasn't awake yet, it was time she got up.

Wet grass soaked his sneakers, and small leaves clung to them as he crossed the lawns.

Nobody on Emily's street was up this early on a Sunday morning, that was clear. A dog barked once, somewhere in the distance, and then it was quiet again. The sun lifted over the treetops, gilding everything it touched with gold.

No lights showed in her windows, and he didn't see any stirring behind the curtains. If he rang the bell, he'd rouse the whole house.

He searched in the flower bed for a handful of pebbles, feeling like the kid who'd thrown gravel at his love's window for one last good-night. He fingered the pebbles, told himself he was an idiot, and tossed one toward the window of what he guessed was Emily's bedroom.

Nothing. Either she didn't hear, or she wasn't in there. He threw another one.

This time he got results. The curtain ruffled and she stared down at him, eyes startled. She turned away, then reappeared, fastening a bathrobe at her throat.

He motioned raising the window. She shook her head at him, half smiling, then pushed up the sash.

"What are you doing?" Her whisper floated down to him.

He grinned. "Saying good morning."

"Good morning." She glanced from side to side, as if expecting an irate neighbor to demand they be quiet.

"No good." He shook his head. "I can't say a proper good morning from this distance. Come on out."

"I can't do that." She clutched the robe tighter. "The boys are still asleep, and I'm not even dressed."

"So come out in your robe. No one's going to see you."

"I can't!" She looked shocked at the thought. "For goodness' sake, I can't run around outside in my robe."

"Why not?" He lifted an eyebrow. He suspected he already knew the answer to that one. "Still afraid of what people will think, Emily?"

"I…" Something, maybe a noise behind her, made her turn. Then she turned back toward him, putting her hands on the window frame. "The boys are awake. I have to get them ready for Sunday school." She smiled. "I'll see you at church. You can say good morning there."

That was Emily, too worried about what everyone else thought to think about what she wanted for herself. He shouldn't blame her for that. Maybe it was part of what she needed to survive in a small town.

Later, seated beside Emily and the boys in the sanctuary, it occurred to him that once again Carmichael wasn't in church. That was odd enough to be noteworthy. In fact, he'd only seen the man two or three times in the last week, even though they were finalizing something of crucial importance.

Maybe Carmichael's absence was for the best, given how he felt about the man. As well as how Carmichael felt about him, for that matter. He'd had the distinct impression James could barely stand to be in the same room with him.

It was a good thing the rest of the family didn't feel the same way. David leaned against his arm as the pastor mounted the pulpit, and Trey smiled at him. There was a certain softness to Emily's smile, too, that hadn't been there before. It was as if she'd come to some conclusion about him, or about their relationship.

He fixed his gaze on Reverend Hayes, trying to concentrate. That was safer than thinking about a relationship with Emily that wasn't going to be.

Not that the minister's text was particularly restful, at least not for him. *Bear with each other and forgive whatever grievance you may have against one another.*

His mouth tightened. He'd much rather hear a sermon today about justice, because justice was about to be done. James Carmichael might benefit from hearing that, too.

He listened, mind half on the sermon, half on Emily. No, he had to be honest, his attention was far more on Emily. What would they do today? She'd promised him the afternoon, but it had to be something the boys would enjoy, too.

He broached the subject as soon as they reached her front porch. "Where would you like to go today? You name it."

There was a quick exchange of glances between Emily and the boys, and he could see they'd discussed it already.

"How would you feel about a picnic? It's a gorgeous day, and this nice weather isn't going to last forever."

"We could go to the state park," Trey said.

"And go hiking," David added. "You like to hike, don't you, Nick?"

He hadn't pictured anything quite so energetic as tramping through the woods. "Is that really what you want? We could drive into the city, if you'd rather."

"A picnic sounds great." Emily gave him the smile that would melt a heart of stone. "If that's okay with you."

He touched her hand. "Your choice."

"A picnic, then. We'll change and get the food ready, and meet you back here in about an hour."

"Not quite. You work all week and do the cooking, too. Today you get a rest. I'll take care of the food." He headed for the car before she could protest. "Back in half an hour."

Actually it took a little longer than that to change his clothes and then stock up on fried chicken and the fixings, but he was soon back at Emily's. The twins were hanging on the porch rail and came running to the car at the sight of him.

"Mom, come on!" Trey shouted. "Nick's here."

He opened the car door for the boys to pile into the back. If Emily hoped to keep their little excursion from the neighbors, it wasn't going to work.

She came hurrying out the door, a red thermos jug swinging from one hand. At his look, she gave an apologetic smile.

"I thought you might not remember drinks, and the refreshment stand at the park is so expensive."

Emily shouldn't have to worry about the cost of soft drinks for her kids. An irrational anger toward Jimmy filled him. Jimmy shouldn't have left her in this position, dependent on his father and unable to tell him what she needed. He'd like to tell the old man that himself.

But he couldn't. He held the door for Emily, then slipped behind the wheel. She'd made her feelings clear, and he respected that. He checked the twins in the rearview mirror, making sure they both had seat belts fastened. And what he'd said to Emily was true. He'd never want to be the one to destroy the boys' image of their father.

"Ready?" He glanced at Emily, and she nodded. "We're off, then."

Off on their last time together, a little voice in his head insisted. He had to savor every moment and put all thoughts of business aside. Once Emily and the twins knew what was going to happen to the mill, they wouldn't want to be within twenty yards of him. This time when he went away, he wouldn't be coming back.

"Thank you, Mrs. Carson, that will be all."

Emily watched as her father-in-law's housekeeper slipped through the swinging door to the kitchen. James Carmichael had to be the last person in town to have a full-time housekeeper. She couldn't imagine what he'd do without Mrs. Carson to keep him in order and produce meals like the one they'd just finished.

Trey caught her eye and grinned at the remains of the coq au vin on his plate. She suppressed a return smile, knowing exactly what he was thinking. He'd enjoyed that cold fried chicken at the park with Nick far more than the elaborate meal at his grandfather's table.

At least, thank goodness, they'd gotten through this with no spills. Something about the mahogany table and lace tablecloth usually brought on such nervousness that they seldom got through Sunday night dinner without one or the other twin knocking over the milk.

James cleared his throat, as if about to start a board meeting. She glanced at him, registering his pallor and the way he leaned on the table.

"Would you like us to leave early?" she said impulsively. "I'm sure you're tired, and with the surgery coming up on Tuesday, you need your rest."

He stiffened. "I am not in the least tired. And I particularly want to speak with you and my grandsons about something."

Trey and David immediately looked apprehensive, as if examining their consciences for some misdeed. She discovered she was clenching her fists on the arms of the ornate mahogany chair and deliberately relaxed them. Sunday night dinner was often uncomfortable, but it wasn't an ordeal. She should be happy James wanted his family around him tonight. He'd already told her he didn't want her to come to the hospital once he'd been admitted.

"Is something wrong, Grandfather?" Trey, of course, was the one to muster up the courage to ask.

"Not at all." Her father-in-law looked at him with as much softness as he produced for anyone. He turned his gaze to Emily. "Do they know I'm going into the hospital?"

She nodded. "I thought it best they know ahead of time."

"I see. Well, perhaps that makes it easier." He divided a gaze between the boys, and they seemed to move a little closer together.

"As I told your mother a few days ago, I've been revising my will." His look sharpened. "You do know what a will is, don't you?"

Her heart sank. She'd hoped he'd forgotten this nonsense.

"Sure we do," Trey said, but his expression said he wasn't sure.

"It's a piece of paper where you write down who you want to have what if you die," David explained.

"Maybe we should write one down." Trey wiggled on his seat. "I could say that you get my bike and my soccer ball. But you have to promise—"

"It's highly unlikely that you need a will just now," his grandfather interrupted. "On the other hand...well, let's say that at my age it's important to have your business affairs in order."

She couldn't let this go on. "I really don't think either of the boys need to know this. Why don't we drop the subject?"

James gave her a frosty look. "I have a responsibility to them. I want them to hear my decision from me."

Trey propped his elbows on the table, apparently forgetting tonight's lecture on table manners, delivered in the car on the way over. "What decision, Grandfather?"

"I've decided that I don't want to split up my share of the mill or the other property I own." He frowned. "I don't suppose you'll understand, but I've always believed it's safer to keep property together."

The twins' foreheads wrinkled, as if they were trying their best to follow his statement.

"Well, now." Even James seemed a little uncomfortable under those unblinking stares. "I've made a decision to leave everything to Trey, since he's the elder of the two of you. Do you understand? This doesn't mean I don't care about you, David. But I feel—"

"No."

James stopped, staring at Trey. "What did you say?"

Trey slid off his chair and stood very straight. "No, thank you, sir."

A flush of color came into James's waxen face. "Trey, you don't understand. This is a complex business matter."

"I understand. You want to give me more than you give David. That's not fair. So I don't want it."

She thought her heart might burst with pride in her son. Pride, and something else. Shame, maybe, that Trey had more courage than she did. "Thank you, Trey. I'm proud of you."

"Emily, I don't think—"

For the first time in their relationship she willingly interrupted her father-in-law. "I think Trey has put it very clearly, James. He's old enough to know what's right. And he speaks for all of us."

She stood up. "Now, I'm sure you should be resting." She went briskly around the table and bent to kiss his cheek. "Good night."

Chapter Thirteen

By the time she got the boys into bed, Emily felt as if she'd run twenty miles. Maybe that wasn't surprising, given the emotional content of the weekend. She paced around the downstairs, unable to relax, still feeling the amazing rightness of Trey's standing up to his grandfather.

Jimmy had never done that. For an instant the thought seemed disloyal, but she forced herself to confront it. All his life, Jimmy had lived in fear of disappointing his father, so much so that it practically guaranteed he would.

How surprising it was that Trey would not only oppose his formidable grandfather, but that he would be willing to give up his inheritance rather than treat his brother unfairly. She touched the photo that stood on the phone table, the two boys smiling up at her.

Maybe this defined the boundaries of the competition she'd sensed between them lately.

When she'd questioned Trey about it on the way home in the car, he'd been nonchalant. But then, he didn't realize exactly what it was he risked giving up.

And then he'd quoted something Nick had told him—something he'd probably garbled a bit about treating people fairly even while you competed with them. When she'd pushed him on it, he'd just shrugged.

"It was guy stuff, Mom," he'd said.

Guy stuff. A hand seemed to clench her heart at that. Her sons needed a man's guidance. They needed a man to look up to, to talk to about the things they didn't want to bring to her. Somehow, in such a short space of time, Nick had stepped into that role.

She'd seen it when they were together at the park. The boys looked to Nick in a way she hadn't expected—a way that actually gave her a momentary vision of the four of them as a family.

She shouldn't let herself think that way. But she couldn't help it. Hope blossomed in spite of her common sense.

She put her hand on the phone. Nick would like to hear what Trey had done. Even more, she'd like to share it with him. Quickly, before she could think about it too much, she dialed his number.

The phone rang six times, seven. Finally she hung up, then walked to the kitchen window. Nick's house was dark. She felt disappointed out of all proportion to the cause that he wasn't there.

Tomorrow. She'd see him at the mill tomorrow, and she'd tell him then.

There was a different atmosphere at the mill. She could sense it the moment she walked through the door the next day. The heightened tension wafted from Betty, behind the receptionist's desk, who looked unusually efficient and busier than she had in years.

Emily stopped at the counter, lifting her eyebrows. "What's going on?"

Betty put her palm over the receiver of the phone. "They're here," she whispered. "A whole team of people from Ex Corp."

"I see." Well, she'd known the transition team would be arriving this week, but she hadn't expected it so early. They must have come into town last night, and that was why Nick had been out. "Is Mr. O'Neill in his office?"

Betty shrugged. "He went up, but he had a couple of people with him. I don't know where they are right now."

This was a place of business, and she had work to do. She went quickly down the hall toward her office. She definitely shouldn't be thinking about how much she was looking forward to seeing Nick again. Or about how special their afternoon with the boys had been.

She paused outside the office they'd assigned to Nick, but the lights were off. Presumably he was somewhere in the building with the people from Ex Corp.

She turned the knob and went in. She scribbled a quick note, saying she'd like to speak with him, and left it folded on his desk. That certainly wasn't compromising or unprofessional, was it? The only unprofessional thing was the way her hand lingered for a moment on the back of his chair.

Back in her office she switched on the computer and brought up on screen the brochure she'd been working on, but her mind refused to concentrate. She spun her chair, looking out at the mill yard. Probably everyone in the building felt the same distraction right now. Change was in the air.

She picked up the phone. Perhaps Betty knew something by now.

"I understand they've all gone up to Mr. Carmichael's office. I don't know why." Betty sounded disappointed that that particular piece of news had escaped her. "Do you want me to ring there?"

"No, thanks, Betty. I'll just go up myself."

She had every right to go up to her father-in-law's office, after all. And if she happened to catch Nick on his way out...well, that would be a coincidence.

But when she entered the secretary's office, it was clear she'd missed him again. The door to James's office stood open, and it was empty.

"Martha, is my father-in-law around?"

Martha Rand didn't turn from the filing cabinet that seemed to be occupying her attention. "He left a few minutes ago, on his way home."

With his surgery scheduled for the next day, that made sense.

"What about Mr. O'Neill? Has he been here?"

Martha slammed the file drawer, the sound shocking in the quiet office. "He was here." She turned around, and Emily realized that her eyes were red-rimmed from crying.

"Martha!" She took a step toward the woman. "What is it? What's wrong?"

"Don't you know?" Martha looked at her strangely. "Do you really not know?"

A shiver of panic swept down her spine. "Know what? What's going on? Is it James?"

Martha shook her head slowly. "It's the mill. Those people from Ex Corp just announced it. They're closing the mill. Carmichael Mills isn't going to exist any longer."

"I don't like being taken by surprise, that's all." Nick glared across his desk at Josh, still dapper and bright-eyed after the trip from New York last night and an early meeting this morning. "You should have told me you were going to drop the bomb today."

Josh shrugged, leaning back in the padded armchair and inspecting his manicured nails. "Listen, old buddy, what difference does it make when we told them? We both knew it would come out soon."

Nick's hands, pressed against the desktop, clenched into fists. "The difference is that you didn't tell me first, *old buddy*. You made it look as if I'd planned it that way, when I didn't know a thing about it."

"Wake up and smell the coffee." Josh abandoned the casual pose and leaned forward, narrow face intent. "We both knew what was going to happen to Carmichael Mills when the merger went through. It was what you wanted, too, remember?"

"I wanted—" He stopped, knowing what it was he wanted. He wanted to talk to Emily, to explain, to tell her this wasn't about her.

Josh stood. "You wanted what? Revenge? Well, you got it. Be happy."

For an instant he just stared at Josh. The man was right. He'd gotten what he wanted, what he'd come to Mannington to do. So why wasn't it enough?

Emily's face, bright-eyed with laughter over something the twins had done, flashed in his mind. Emily. Emily was the reason the vengeance he'd longed for had turned to ashes in his mouth. He loved her.

The idea was as astonishing as it was true. The truth of it settled into his heart. He loved her. Maybe he'd never stopped loving her. And he had to see her, had to explain...

The door burst open. Emily stood there, her amber eyes blazing, her face white.

Josh looked from Emily to him, then waved his hand in an awkward gesture. "Maybe I'd better..."

"Yes, maybe you had better." He had to talk to Emily, and he certainly couldn't do it with Josh there.

Josh sidled past Emily and closed the door. They were alone.

"Is it true?" Her gaze struck him like a blow.

"Emily, please." He went around the desk toward her, mind racing. How could he make her understand? "Come and sit down."

"I don't want to sit down. Is it true?"

All the softness was gone. This was an Emily he hadn't seen before. He wouldn't be able to escape or evade those questions. Nothing but the truth would do.

"I don't know what you've heard, but it's not as bad as you think."

"I've heard that the mill is closing." That soft chin had never looked so uncompromising. "Is it true?"

"Yes." There wasn't any other answer.

For an instant her eyes seemed to blank him out, as if she couldn't bear to look at him. When she did look at him again, those warm amber eyes were stone cold. "That's really why you came here, isn't it? To close the mill."

"Ex Corp is closing the mill, not me." That was a cop-out, and he knew it. "Look, this is a business decision. We can fill the orders more economically from our plant in Tennessee, that's all. It would take more to modernize this place than it's worth."

"So that's it?" Her anger blazed at him. "You

throw two hundred people out of work because it's more economical?''

"We're not throwing them onto the street. We'll offer jobs at our other plants to as many as we can."

She rejected that with a sharp cut of her hand. "What if people don't want to leave? Mannington is their home."

Why was she so obsessed with this place? "Mannington's not the only town in the world. Maybe some of them will be better off elsewhere."

"It will kill this town." Her eyes clouded with pain. "It will kill James."

"Carmichael." He crossed the space between them and glared down at her. "Is that all you can think about? Let me tell you something about James Carmichael."

Her face softened slightly. "Nick, I know you dislike him because of his dispute with your father. But that's no reason…"

"Dispute? Is that what you call it?"

A flush rose in her pale cheeks. "All right, your father was fired. After the theft was discovered, James thought he had good reason."

"My father was framed. There never was a theft." He threw the words at her. "That was the threat Carmichael used to force him to leave, just because he tried to unionize the place, to force almighty James Carmichael to give his employees decent wages and health benefits. And not content with framing my father and running him out of town, Carmichael kept him from ever getting a decent job again." Anger burned along his veins. "That's your precious father-in-law for you."

She went pale again. "I don't believe you."

"No, I don't suppose you would, any more than the rest of this town would. But now the scales are balanced."

"Vengeance, Nick?"

"Justice."

She shook her head. "I don't see any justice in throwing two hundred people out of work to right a wrong you think was done to you."

Something hardened in him at that. She was never going to understand. "It's my father he destroyed, not me."

"No." Her voice was soft. "You're doing a good job of that all by yourself."

"Most people would say I'm pretty successful."

"Most people wouldn't look inside you and see the pain. Or the damage you're doing to yourself with this…this vendetta."

For a moment he couldn't speak. At a time like this only Emily would care about the damage she imagined he was doing to his soul.

"Emily." He caught her hand, and his voice roughened. "I'm sorry I couldn't warn you what was coming. But you've got to look past the moment. I know change is difficult, but this was inevitable. If it hadn't been Ex Corp today, it would have been somebody else next year."

"You don't know that." Pain etched itself between her brows. "And anybody would have been better than you."

"If I hadn't come, we wouldn't have seen each other again." He tried to warm her cold hand in his. "If I hadn't come, I might never have known I love you."

"Love?" She winced, as if the word had been a blow.

"Try and understand. This is going to be better for everybody in the long run. You and the boys don't have to stay in Mannington any longer. You don't have to be dependent on Carmichael. We can build a life for ourselves somewhere else."

She pulled her hand away. "On the ashes of other people's lives?"

He was losing her; he could see it in her eyes. But he couldn't lose what he'd never had. "Do you love me, Emily?"

She flinched. "I thought I did. But I guess I didn't even know you."

She walked out, closing the door quietly behind her.

Emily managed to preserve that deadly calm across the hall to her own office. Safely inside, she closed the door and leaned back against it. Then she pressed both hands against her chest.

Funny, that the pain really could feel as if her heart were broken. As if, if she could look at it, she'd see the tiny separate pieces of what had been her love for Nick.

The phone was ringing. She crossed to the desk, took the receiver off the hook, put it on the blotter. Then she sank into the chair and buried her face in her hands.

How could this happen, Lord? How could Nick do this?

The trouble was, she knew the answer. He could do it because of what he believed had happened to his father. He could do it because his heart was so eaten up with revenge that there wasn't room for anything else.

Like love. She winced at the word. She loved him. She couldn't turn it off and pretend it hadn't happened. Maybe she'd always loved him, in that special place in her heart that was reserved for her first love. Then he'd come back, and she'd thought, she'd hoped....

And now he'd betrayed them all. She tried not to think of how she'd talk to the boys about this. The man they'd begun to see as a hero had turned on them.

Lord, he doesn't know what he's doing to himself. He's destroying himself, and he doesn't even realize it. Even if what he believes about James is true, Nick is hurting himself far more than he'll ever hurt James.

She straightened, massaging her temples. All the lights on her phone were blinking now. Clearly the word was out. People were calling her, expecting her to have answers, and she didn't.

She felt a brief spurt of annoyance at James, who'd gone home and left her to deal with this. At least he might have talked with her so that she'd have some idea what to say to people.

She shoved back away from the desk. She had to see him. She had to find out how he expected her to handle this. The whole town depended on the mill, and they'd expect answers.

And she had to find out the truth about Nick's father. She put her hand lightly on the photo of the twins. If their grandfather really had done such a terrible thing... Her mind reeled at the consequences.

She had to know the truth. Whatever it was, she'd find a way to deal with it, for the boys' sakes. But first, she had to know.

More than an hour later she argued her way past the nurse and reached the door of James's room. She'd gone to the house first, only to find that he'd headed directly for the hospital to check in for his surgery. She'd driven there, seeming to feel the accusing gazes of people on the streets as the news spread up one side of Main Street and down the other.

She took a deep breath, sent up a silent prayer for guidance and opened the door.

James was tucked up on the high hospital bed, his maroon silk robe contrasting with the white bedclothes. His gaze stabbed accusingly at her.

"I told you I didn't want you to come to the hospital."

"I had to come." She approached him, some of her determination ebbing as she saw how white and strained he looked. "The mill—did you know this was going to happen?"

Anger tightened his pale lips. "Know? Of course I didn't know. Do you think I'd have agreed to any deal if I'd realized what they had in mind? This was all O'Neill's doing." Two bright spots of color showed on his cheeks. "I should have suspected the moment I heard he was their representative. He's wanted to get back at us for years. Just like his father."

"That's why he did it." Somehow she had to get to the truth. It was the only thing that would help any of them. "Because of his father. Because of what he believes you did to his father."

James stared at her, blue eyes frosty. "I don't know what you mean. The man was a thief. What would you expect me to do?"

"Nick says he wasn't—that it was all a lie."

"What would you expect him to say? It's all nonsense."

That came out with his usual assurance, but his gaze slid away from hers, focusing instead on the tile floor. A cold hand seemed to clasp her heart.

"He's right, isn't he?" Her breath caught, threatening to choke her. "He's right. His father wasn't a thief."

"That's nonsense, sheer...nonsense." His voice faltered on the last word, and he leaned back against the pillow. His eyes closed, then opened again. His hand moved, restlessly smoothing the sheet that covered him.

"James." She took his hand, holding it firmly. "Tell me the truth. I have a right to know."

She thought he wouldn't answer. Then his head moved slowly from side to side, and she seemed to feel the defiance seep out of him.

"Tell me," she said again, more softly. "At a time like this, be honest with me."

"I just wanted to be rid of him." His voice came out in a whisper. "That's all. He was causing trouble, making demands we couldn't meet. He was trying to unionize the place, but a union back then would have ruined us."

She waited, dreading to hear the rest of it. *Oh, Lord...* She wasn't even sure what to pray.

His hand moved feebly in hers. "Donovan handled it. I didn't tell him what to do. Mack Donovan, the foreman, you remember him."

Her memory produced an image of the wiry, graying foreman who'd retired years ago and left Mannington. "I remember. What does he have to do with it?"

"He said he'd take care of it." His hand trembled slightly, and the sign of weakness hurt her. "When O'Neill was caught, I wondered. But I didn't do anything. I should have, but I didn't. He left, and my people were safe from him. I told myself that was all that mattered.''

''After he left, what did you do about him?'' The rest of Nick's accusation couldn't be left unanswered.

''Do?'' His gaze focused on her, and a little strength seemed to come back into his voice. ''I didn't do anything.''

''You didn't try to keep him from getting other jobs?''

''Of course not. I don't even know where he went. I just thought I'd heard the last of him.'' His mouth twisted in an attempt at a smile. ''I should have known better. Your sins always find you out, one way or another.''

She couldn't think of anything to say to that. It was true, and unfortunately a lot of other people were going to pay for this particular misdeed.

''What are we going to do?'' Her fingers tightened on his cold ones.

''Nothing.'' His voice failed on the word, and he struggled to repeat it. ''Nothing to do. Tell them— tell them I'm sorry.''

She started to move away, but he held her. ''Wait. Emily, tell my attorney to come in. Right away, before the surgery.''

''Can't it wait? You should be resting.'' He seemed too weak to face an operation.

''No. I've decided.'' A ghost of a smile crossed his face. ''Trey was right. I'm going to sign everything over to you now. I know you'll do what's right for the boys and for the mill.''

It was a burden she didn't want, but she didn't have a choice. There wasn't anyone else. ''I'll do my best.''

''One more thing,'' he whispered. ''If I come through tomorrow, I'll give O'Neill my apology. I don't suppose he'll forgive me, but I'll try.''

She nodded, turning to the door. Too late, that was all she could think. It was too little, too late, for all of them.

Chapter Fourteen

The rest of her day passed in a haze of misery. She went back to the office, because someone from the family had to be there. The phone never stopped ringing. Everyone wanted to know if it was true, wanted details, wanted someone to blame, wanted to be comforted.

Ironically, the people suffering the most seemed to be those who were receiving the offers at Ex Corp's other plants. They were torn between staying and facing an uncertain future and going, giving up homes and familiar surroundings for the unknown. She choked down her own pain and tried to listen, knowing she didn't have answers.

Nick, how could you do this? How could you hurt so many people?

There didn't seem to be an answer to that, either.

The phone rang yet again, and Emily reached for

it, trying to compose her heart to listen. But this person didn't want sympathy. It was one of the Ex Corp people.

"Josh Trent here, Ms. Carmichael. I wanted to inform you that Mr. Donaldson, our vice president for acquisitions, will be here tomorrow. He'd like to make arrangements for the final disposition of the plant and its fittings."

The words had a funereal sound. "I see."

"He'd like to meet with you...well, let's see. Not tomorrow, he'll be too busy. The next day at ten, if that's convenient, in Mr. Carmichael's former office."

It was less a question than a command.

"At ten, then."

Somehow, between now and then, she'd have to figure out if there was anything she could use to push Ex Corp into doing better by the workers. She didn't think an appeal to their better nature would help. Before she could stop it, her mind flew to Nick. Since he'd come back, she'd begun, without even realizing it, to count on him. Now she knew she couldn't, but some small part of her heart still wanted to.

By the time she went home, she was emotionally and physically exhausted. It didn't help to hear the twins coming up the walk from school in the midst of a full-blown quarrel.

"You're a dummy, that's all," Trey yelled.

"I don't believe it." David dropped his backpack

on the floor, his mouth set in a firm line as he frowned at his brother. "Nick wouldn't."

Her heart sank. There wouldn't be any respite from what was going on here, either. The only way to handle it was to face it—her sons deserved honesty. She sat down, feeling as if her legs wouldn't hold her up any longer.

Please, Lord. Give me the right words. They've begun to care for him, too.

"Come here, guys." She held out her hands, drawing them to either side of her on the couch. "Okay, now tell me what's going on."

"We heard the mill's going to close." David looked up at her, small face troubled. "It's not, is it, Mommy?"

"I'm afraid so." She put her arm around him.

Trey kicked his heels against the sofa. "Some of the kids said it's Nick's fault. That he did it."

She could sense the pleading under his words. He wanted her to say that it wasn't true, that the person he looked up to wouldn't do that.

"He didn't, did he?" David's eyes filled with tears. "He wouldn't do that."

Where were the right words to help them deal with the fact that their hero was tarnished?

"Nick works for the company that bought part of the mill, and they've decided to close it. It's not just his decision. It's his boss's decision, too."

"But couldn't Grandfather keep our part of the mill

open?'' Trey offered the idea as if it would solve everything.

"I'm afraid it doesn't work that way, Trey." She smoothed silky hair out of his eyes. "You see, the person who has the biggest share gets to decide for everyone. And that's Ex Corp."

"Nick could have stopped them if he wanted to." Trey's mouth set in a stubborn line. "I hate him."

David leaned against her. "I thought he was our friend." A tear trickled down his cheek.

She drew them both close. "I know." Her arms couldn't shield them from this kind of pain. "I thought so, too."

It seemed much later than nine o'clock by the time the boys were finally settled for the night. Emily walked slowly into her bedroom. Maybe she ought to go to bed herself and let sleep block out the terrible events of the day. Or maybe she'd just dream about it, over and over.

Nick's class ring still lay in her dresser drawer. She took it out, trying to remember how she'd felt about the boy who'd given it to her.

She'd loved him, at least as much as a fifteen-year-old could understand the word. Her heart had, she'd been sure, broken when he'd gone away.

She held the ring against her cheek, feeling the cool, hard metal.

And then he'd come back, and she'd loved him again. She hadn't intended to, hadn't even known it was happening until it was too late. She loved him, and he'd betrayed them all, including himself.

He wasn't the same person. That was what she had to face. The fact that she loved him didn't change that. She'd probably continue loving him for a long time, but she couldn't be with the person he was now. He'd let his bitterness and anger turn him into a man who didn't even recognize the wrong he was doing.

The tears threatened to overflow, and she sank down on her knees beside her bed, burying her face in her hands.

Lord, show me how to deal with this. Show me what to do, because I just don't know.

She took a deep breath, then another, feeling the panic dissolve slowly.

Forgiveness. That was what was wrong with Nick—he hadn't been able to forgive. If she didn't want to confront the same bitterness he lived with, somehow she had to forgive.

I don't think I can forgive him in my own strength, Lord. But I know Your strength is sufficient. So I'll forgive him and trust in You to make it so.

Comfort seeped through her, erasing the tension and easing the pain. She should have learned by now that relying on her own strength was a recipe for disaster. But there was always One she could lean on.

She prayed for the boys and for James and for all those who would be affected by the mill's closing. Then, finally feeling at peace, she prayed for Nick.

* * *

On Tuesday afternoon Nick paused outside the door to what had been Carmichael's office. Donaldson had taken it over when he arrived that morning, brisk and full of determination to clean things up and move on.

Mrs. Rand still sat at the secretary's desk, talking on the telephone. When she caught Nick's gaze on her she cut the conversation short, then looked up at him, eyes icy.

"I trust you don't object to a brief personal call. I wanted to check with the hospital."

"Hospital?" For some reason his mind leaped to Emily and the boys. "Who's in the hospital?"

She sniffed. "Mr. Carmichael, of course."

He could only stare at her for a moment. "I didn't know. What happened?"

"His surgery was this morning." Then, apparently recognizing the blank look he gave her, she went on. "I thought you knew. He had to have heart surgery."

"No, I didn't know." Emily hadn't told him. But then, she wouldn't. He was the enemy. "How is he?"

Mrs. Rand contrived to look a bit stiffer. "I understand he came through the surgery fairly well." She paused. "That was Mrs. Carmichael."

He pictured Emily waiting at the hospital, waiting for word, worrying about Carmichael, about the mill, about the people who were going to be unemployed. She'd probably been worrying about Carmichael's health for days, in addition to everything else. In addition to the burdens he'd put on her.

He didn't particularly like this train of thought. He ought to...what? His mind jeered at him. Send flowers? Neither Carmichael nor Emily would appreciate that. He ought to leave well enough alone. He'd done what he came to Mannington to do, and the only favor he could do Emily right now was to stay away from her.

But he couldn't. He didn't want to. He wanted to try, one more time, to explain.

He glanced at his watch. He had a couple more hours of work to do before he could leave. Maybe by that time Emily would be home from the hospital. He could stop by the house and tell her... His mind ran up against a blank wall at that point. Tell her what?

He still hadn't decided by the time he left the office. He just knew he wasn't going to leave Mannington without trying to see her again.

He was so occupied with his thoughts that he didn't notice the group of men gathered in the parking lot until he was close to them.

"O'Neill." Ken Moore, Lorna's husband, looked considerably more threatening than he had that night at the fairgrounds. "We need to talk."

"Oh?" Nick sized up the distance to his car, the distance back to the building. "Looks like you brought some friends along to help you talk."

Ken's large fists clenched. "I don't need any help. I just want to know one thing. Why? What did we do to you?"

For a moment he was tempted to be honest. You

branded my father a thief—you and the rest of this town.

But he wouldn't give them the satisfaction. "It's business. Ex Corp decided this plant wasn't worth the money to modernize."

"Ex Corp decided? Or you decided?"

He bit back a sharp retort. Nobody would thank him for starting a brawl in the company parking lot.

"It was a corporate decision."

"Corporate." Ken took a step closer, close enough so that Nick could see the pain as well as anger in the man's eyes. "What kind of corporation takes a man's livelihood away from him?"

"Look, we're trying to offer jobs to as many people as possible." He knew Ken was one of those who'd received the offer; he'd made sure of that. Unfortunately he'd also heard what his answer had been.

"We don't want your jobs!" Ken's voice rose. "We want our jobs. We want our town back the way it was before you came along."

Nick's fists tightened. He didn't want to fight the man, but he'd protect himself if it came to that.

Ken seemed to see the movement. For a long moment he stared at Nick, then his hands opened, gesturing as if to push something away.

"Forget it," he said. "We're not going to take you on, O'Neill. We have wives and kids to take care of, and you're not worth the trouble." The contempt in his voice stung. He turned away, and the group of men sidled back with him.

Nick let out a breath he didn't realize he'd been holding.

Ken looked back over his shoulder. "Too bad Emily and her kids didn't have someone to take care of them."

The verbal blow stung as much as a punch would have. Emily and her boys. Obviously people had been talking. For the first time he understood why that bothered her so much.

The men moved away, not looking at him. So he was back to being a pariah in this town. Well, he'd been there before. He could deal with it.

Trouble was, now that he had his revenge on Carmichael, he didn't seem to feel the satisfaction he'd expected. He didn't seem to feel anything at all.

"Thank you, Doctor. I'll be in again sometime tomorrow." Emily hung up the phone and looked at the twins, bookends on either side of Alison, who'd come to play. "Good news." She tried to look cheerful. "The doctor says your grandfather is doing much better now."

They didn't look convinced.

"Are you sure?" Trey said. "Somebody said at school Grandfather might be going to die."

She ruffled his hair. "Who are you going to believe, his doctor or somebody at school?"

Trey grinned. "Okay. I guess Brett didn't know what he was talking about. Sometimes he doesn't."

"Right." She set three glasses of juice in front of

them. ''Maybe in a few days he'll feel well enough that you can go to see him. In the meantime…''

The doorbell rang. Her heart pumped into overdrive at the sound. Silly. Maybe it was a measure of how much stress she'd been under that the least noise should set her nerves on edge.

The twins stampeded toward the door.

''I'll get it!'' Trey yelled.

''No, me.''

That brought a smile as she followed them. It sounded as if things were getting back to normal, at least a little.

The smile faded when she saw who was stepping into her living room. Nick.

The boys just stood, staring at him.

She didn't have anything to say to him. And whatever she did say, she didn't want the twins to hear.

''Trey and David, you and Alison take your juice out to the back porch, please.''

Trey's small chin jutted out. ''We want to talk to Nick.''

David nodded.

''No.'' That came out sharply, but it couldn't be helped. Maybe she hadn't protected anyone else from Nick's revenge, but she was going to shield her children. ''Do what I say, now.''

Their faces wore identically startled expressions, but they went. She didn't turn back to Nick until she heard the slam of the back door.

"You were a little hard on them, weren't you?" His voice was mild, his deep blue eyes questioning.

"I don't think that's your concern. Why are you here?" She longed for a protection from his intent gaze. If he looked too hard, he just might see how much she was hurting.

"I…" His hand moved in a small, almost pleading, motion. For once he seemed to be at a loss for words. "I wanted to talk to you."

Please make him go away before I let him know how much I care.

"I think we've said everything there is to say."

He shook his head in a characteristically impatient gesture, a lock of black hair falling over his forehead. "Emily, look, first of all, I'm sorry about your father-in-law's health problems. I didn't know. How is he doing?"

A welcome spurt of anger went through her at that. "Do you care?"

"Oddly enough, I do." He shrugged. "I don't know why. Maybe it's your influence, Emily. You care about everybody."

She pushed away a fresh spasm of pain. It would be tempting to believe she could change him, but she didn't. "He's come through the surgery all right. He's very weak, but if there are no complications, the doctor is hopeful."

"If I'd known you were carrying that burden, along with everything else…" He stopped, as if he didn't know what to say.

She shook her head. "It wouldn't have made a difference, Nick. Admit it. You were so bent on revenge that nothing would make a difference." There was something else, something he had a right to hear, whether she wanted to say it or not. "Maybe you were right."

"Why do you say that?" His gaze sharpened.

She took a deep breath and forced herself to look at him. "I talked to James before his surgery. Asked him about what you told me."

"Did he admit it?"

"He said he wanted to be rid of your father—to protect the mill and his workers. He believed the union would cost too much, put them out of business. He suspected the foreman rigged the charges against your father, but he didn't do anything about it. He knows that makes him guilty. He's sorry."

Bitterness twisted Nick's mouth. "A little late now. Isn't it?"

"Nick, don't." His emotion seemed to spark her own pain. Didn't he see what he was doing to himself? "You have what you wanted. You've gotten your revenge. Is it enough? Does it make you happy?"

The door banged, as if emphasizing the question. Trey raced into the room.

One look at his white face told her something was very wrong.

"Mommy, come quick! Alison fell out of the tree." He grabbed her hand. "She won't wake up!"

Chapter Fifteen

Nick raced after Emily and Trey, through the kitchen, across the porch, across the lawn. Emily got to the still figure first, reaching for the child, with him right behind her.

"Don't!" He caught her hand in his. "Careful. Better not move her."

Some of the panic left Emily's eyes at his tone, and she nodded. She reached out carefully to put her fingers on Alison's neck.

"Her pulse is strong." Her voice seemed to catch a little. She leaned closer and listened to her breathing. "She's breathing all right, too," she added.

"Looks as if she hit her head when she fell." He'd already seen the rapidly darkening lump on her temple. "Better call for an ambulance. I don't think we should risk moving her without a backboard."

She nodded again. "Stay with her. I'll be right back." She ran toward the house.

His mind went through the little first aid he knew. It wasn't much, but he was sure they were right not to move her. He could understand Emily's first instinct to gather the child into her arms, though. It seemed all wrong for a live wire like Alison to lie so still.

David edged a little closer, his knee bumping Alison's arm.

"Don't touch her," Nick cautioned.

The boy looked stricken at his words.

"She'll be all right, son." He touched David's shoulder lightly. "We just don't want to move her until the ambulance comes and they can do it right."

David's eyes were huge. "Can't I do something?"

"Why don't you run and get a blanket to keep her warm. Can you do that?"

"Sure." David scrambled to his feet, carefully avoiding Alison. "Right away."

Trey knelt next to Nick. His small body shook with a choked sob, and his hand crept forward until he was just touching Alison's sleeve. "It's my fault."

"Why do you say that?" He kept his voice carefully neutral.

"I dared her. Mommy always says not to dare people, but I dared her to stand on the limb. It's my fault she got hurt." His face crumpled, another sob escaping.

"Trey..." Careful, careful. Don't say the wrong

thing. "You didn't mean for your friend to get hurt. It was an accident."

He clasped the boy's shoulder in a reassuring grip. Trey jerked away as if he'd struck him.

"What do you know about it?" Trey's grief changed suddenly to anger. "You hurt your friends, and you didn't even care!"

It was like being kicked in the heart. The expression on Trey's face weighed him, judged him and found him guilty. And there wasn't a thing Nick could say that would make this all right.

Emily hurried back, closely followed by David, arms filled with a blanket he'd probably ripped from his bed.

"The ambulance will be here in a few minutes. I sent a friend to try and find Lorna. She's gone shopping." Her voice trembled a little, but she tucked the blanket over the child with competent hands.

"What about Ken?"

"I don't know where to look for him." She bit her lip. "Maybe Lorna will know."

The wail of the ambulance sent her to her feet. She hurried to the side of the house, waving them in.

Nick drew the boys out of the way as the paramedics examined Alison and slid a backboard under her. Her eyelids fluttered when they moved her, and she tried to say something.

"Mommy?" she whispered.

"It's okay, Alison." Emily moved beside her.

"Mommy will be here soon, and I'll stay with you until she comes."

She glanced at Nick, and he nodded.

"You ride in the ambulance with her. I'll bring the boys and meet you at the emergency room."

She was shaking her head before he got the words out. "I'd rather they stay here. The hospital's no place for them."

"Trust me on this one." He looked meaningfully at Trey. "They need to be there. I'll take good care of them."

She didn't look as if she agreed, but the paramedics were already lifting Alison. "I'll see you there, then." She hurried after them.

The two boys stared at him with identically doubting expressions. Funny, that that look should hurt more than almost anything had since he came back to town.

"Come on." He tried to make it sound routine, tried not to think about how badly hurt the child might be. "My car's in the driveway. We'll be at the hospital before you know it."

Emily backed out of the emergency room cubicle, giving the medical people more room to work. She'd been in this same spot several times with the boys, and it never failed to give her that weak-in-the-knees feeling. Maybe you could only go on being strong as long as you were needed.

She could hear a doctor ordering a CAT scan, and

her stomach seemed to turn over. How badly hurt was
Alison? She'd been unconscious for several
minutes—that couldn't be good.

Father, be with her. Guide the doctor's every move.

Where was Lorna? Judith Wells had promised to
keep looking until she found her, no matter what it
took, and Judith was a woman of her word. She'd
track Lorna down and bring her here, to face…what?

She knew only too well the guilt that Lorna would
feel over not being there when Alison was hurt. It
might be totally irrational, but there wasn't a mother
on earth who wouldn't understand.

She pushed away from the wall and took a few
steps into the lobby. The door swished open and
Lorna charged into the room, heading first for the
desk and then veering when she saw Emily.

"How bad is it?" She clutched Emily's arm.
"Where is she?"

Emily embraced her, feeling her friend tremble in
her arms. "The doctors are with her now. They
haven't told me anything yet. She fell from the tree
and hit her head." Her own guilt kicked in. "Lorna,
I'm sorry. I should have been watching them more
closely."

Lorna shook her head, tears spilling over to be
dashed quickly away. "It's not your fault. She wanted
to go shopping with me, but I thought…"

"It's not your fault, either." She gave Lorna a little
shake. "Make sense. She didn't fall just because you
didn't want to take her shopping this afternoon."

"No, of course not." Lorna brushed away an errant tear and took a deep breath. "Okay. Do I look calm enough to go in now?"

"You're fine." She nodded toward the waiting room. "I'll be out here when you need me."

She watched the white curtain close behind Lorna, heard a soft "Mommy" and wiped away a tear of her own. *Please, Father. Hold this child safe.*

When she turned back to the waiting room, she saw that Nick and the twins had come in. She stood for a moment, watching as they found seats, Nick sitting between the two boys.

She'd depended on him. In that moment of crisis, when life turned upside down all in an instant, she'd counted on Nick in spite of everything he'd done.

And it had felt right. That was the scary thing— how good it had been to rely on his strength, to have another person helping with the responsibility.

Not just another person. She'd thought that often enough in the years since Jimmy died, but she didn't need just any other person. It was Nick she'd leaned on. Nick, with all his flaws, that she'd known instinctively she could trust.

She watched him lean toward David, saying something softly that eased the tension in his small face.

Oh, Nick.

Her throat went tight with anguish. There was so much good in him, so much strength and fortitude. But it was all being eaten away by bitterness, and he didn't even know it.

She swallowed hard, then crossed the waiting room toward them.

"Mommy!" Trey bolted from his seat to meet her halfway. "Is she all right? Did she wake up?"

Emily stroked his hair as she led him back to the others. She sat down, pulling the chair around so that she could face both boys on their level.

"She's waking up a little bit. I heard her say something to her mommy. So that's good."

"Is she all right? Can she go home now?" David wiggled forward on his chair, as if ready to run into the other room and take Alison by the hand.

"Not yet. The doctors are still checking her. They have to do some tests to see how much her head is hurt. Remember the X-ray you had when you fell off your bike, Trey?"

He nodded. "It didn't hurt."

"No, and Alison's tests won't hurt, either. We just have to wait and see what the doctors say."

"Isn't there anything we can do?" Trey grabbed her hand, and she felt his urgency. "I want to do something."

She managed a smile. "I think we'd better pray for her. That's the best thing we can do right now." She held out her hands to the boys.

Trey clasped her hand like a lifeline, but when Nick extended his, Trey drew back in a quick, angry movement. She saw the flicker of pain in Nick's face, immediately masked.

"Trey." At the moment, she cared more what

Trey's anger did to him than to what it did to Nick. "Take Nick's hand, please."

"Don't..." Nick began, but she silenced him with a look.

"I don't want to. He's not our friend anymore."

"Listen to me, Trey. This is important. You can't go to God with a prayer for one person when you're holding a grudge against someone else. Do you understand that? And you have to forgive other people when they do something wrong just as you want God to forgive you."

She watched his face. This was a big spiritual lesson for one so young, but it was one he had to start learning now. He'd probably keep on learning it all his life, just as she had.

Trey stared down at the floor. She thought he was fighting tears, but she didn't move. This one he had to battle out himself.

Finally he looked up. He nodded. Then he held his hand out to Nick.

She closed her eyes. "Dear Father, we bring Alison to You now. We ask that You be with her and heal her. We ask You to guide her doctors and give them wisdom. We ask You to comfort her parents and be with each of us. In Jesus' precious name, Amen."

Nick discovered that the lump in his throat was too big to swallow. If he tried to say anything at all, he might choke or give way to tears. Emily's soft-voiced prayer, the grip of the boys' small hands on his, the thought of little Alison, lying pale and motionless on the ground—it all rolled over him, threatening to knock him flat.

The sound of rushing feet came from the entrance. Ken raced in, his face distraught. Emily moved toward him, and he grasped her outstretched hands.

"Alison?" The naked fear in his voice ripped into Nick's heart.

Nick was probably the last person Ken wanted to see right now.

"Come on, guys." It took an effort to sound normal. "Let's find a soda machine and get everyone something to drink."

He spent as much time as he could on the simple task. When they got back to the waiting room, Ken had vanished, probably into the examining room. Emily stood in the doorway, and he thought she looked a little more relaxed.

"Thank you, Trey." She took the soda can the boy held out to her. "I was with Ken when he spoke to the doctor. Alison has a concussion." She glanced from Trey to David. "That's what happens when you hit your head really hard. They're going to keep her in the hospital for a bit just to watch her, but it looks as if she'll be all right."

"Can we see her?" Trey's tone was pleading. "Please, can we see her? I have to tell her something."

"I don't think they'll want her to have visitors today. Maybe you can make a card for her."

He shook his head, and Nick knew exactly what put that stubborn expression in his eyes. The kid was still blaming himself, and he wouldn't be able to rest until he'd told Alison he was sorry.

"I have to see her. Please, Mom."

He had to think of something that would ease the boy's pain. "Maybe if we wait until they're ready to move her to a room, you can say something to her on the way up." He looked at Emily. "It's important," he said quietly.

He expected her to argue, but she didn't. She just nodded.

"All right. We'll wait."

The boys scurried back to their chairs, as if afraid she might change her mind.

"Is Ken okay?" He seemed to hear the man's voice echoing in his head. *We have wives and kids to take care of.*

Emily's eyes held a question she didn't ask. "He was better as soon as he saw Alison. Not knowing is scary."

"I'd like to…" He let that trail off. Ken wouldn't appreciate hearing anything from him.

"What?" Emily's direct gaze didn't allow equivocation.

He shrugged, suspecting he looked like one of the kids when he'd done something wrong. "I'd like to express my concern, that's all. But under the circumstances, it might be kind of awkward."

She looked at him steadily. "Does that matter, if it's something you should say?"

He didn't doubt she'd apply those same standards to herself. "Maybe not."

"He's gone to the admissions desk to fill out some forms. You can catch up with him there." She nodded down the hallway.

Looked as if Emily wouldn't let him get out of this one. Maybe she was right, and he needed to do this. Maybe it would still the churning that had been going on inside him.

He walked down the green-walled hallway quickly, automatically checking off the signs. When he came to the admissions desk, he saw Ken frowning down at a sheaf of papers. The young woman across the desk looked bored.

She reached across to tap a line on the form with a red-tipped nail. "Right there. You have to put your insurance information on the sheet before we can process the admission."

Nick stopped in his tracks, knowing what Ken was going to say. What he'd have to say.

"Look, I work...worked at the mill. Our insurance has been terminated." Nick recoiled in shock. Had he overheard correctly? Had Ex Corp already terminated the insurance plan? That wasn't supposed to happen so quickly. "But I'll pay." He heard Ken continue. "The doctor says Alison has to be admitted."

"No insurance." She took the paper back, looking less bored. "Does that mean you're unemployed?"

"Yes." Ken sounded as if the word had a bad taste.

"Unemployed. No insurance." She scribbled something on the form. "Are you on welfare?"

"No!"

He could see the vein pulsing in Ken's temple. The man was an inch from exploding.

"Then I'm afraid we'll have to have the money up front. You can't expect the hospital to treat your daughter for free, can you?"

"You…"

He stepped forward before Ken could bring his fist down on the counter.

"You do accept cash, don't you?" Nick pulled out his wallet. "What are the charges going to be?"

Ken whirled, glaring when he saw who was there. "Stay out of this, O'Neill. If it weren't for you, we wouldn't be in this fix."

"Look, I just want to help."

"Help?" His fists clenched. "Get out of my sight before I do something I'll regret. I'd rather panhandle on the street than accept money from you."

Ken spun back to the desk, saying something about writing a check. Nick took a step back, an image blossoming in his mind. His father, ranting about the wrong done to him by Carmichael. Raving that the man was responsible for all their troubles. That he'd rather beg on the street than accept help from the likes of him.

The piercing moment washed away all the excuses, all the rationalizations. He was left facing the stark, hard truth. He'd let his bitterness turn him into the very image of the man he'd hated all these years.

Chapter Sixteen

By the time she walked into the meeting with Donaldson the next morning, Emily felt as if she'd been steamrollered. The events of the past few days, coming so quickly one on top of the other, had left no time to take a breath between them.

At least the news from the hospital was good. Alison's condition had improved, and she'd probably be home tomorrow at the latest. And James was stronger—strong enough, in fact, for him to meet again with his attorney. His shares of the mill had been signed over to her, to manage as she wished for the twins.

Not that she'd be able to do much managing. She glanced at Jefferson Wade, the attorney, as he moved into the office behind her. He hadn't held out much hope that they'd be able to wring any concessions from Donaldson. They didn't, he'd said, have anything left to bargain with.

She sent a quick glance around the office, trying to adjust to the sight of a stranger behind James's desk. Or maybe she was really looking for Nick.

She'd expected he'd try to talk with her again after that trip to the hospital, but he hadn't. He'd simply disappeared.

Not that there'd have been any use in talking again. They didn't have anything to say to each other, and if that left her feeling as if there were a hole in her heart—well, she'd have to get over it. Someday.

Donaldson was tall and balding, with cold, shrewd eyes behind gold-rimmed glasses. He shook hands, gesturing her to a seat with a proprietary air that raised her hackles.

Jefferson Wade gave her a warning glance as he held the chair for her. She knew what he was saying. *Don't offend him. We're not negotiating from a position of power.*

"Now, Ms. Carmichael." Donaldson ruffled a sheaf of papers on the desk in front of him. "I called you here to discuss the final disposition of the mill's equipment before we put the building up for sale."

She had to swallow before she could speak. "I can't imagine that you'll find a buyer very easily."

He shrugged. "That really doesn't concern us. About the equipment..."

"I'd rather talk about the workers." The strength

of her voice surprised her. "How many of our people have been offered new jobs?"

Donaldson's eyes looked like two black marbles. "We've found places for about twenty."

"Twenty out of two hundred?"

"We're not running a charity, Ms. Carmichael."

"But you can't—"

The door swung open, and Donaldson's expression changed, hardening even more, if that were possible.

"O'Neill, you're not needed at this meeting." His voice seemed to carry a warning.

Nick apparently intended to ignore it, if it was a warning. His gaze brushed her coolly, impersonally, and he nodded to her. "Ms. Carmichael. Wade."

A sliver of ice seemed to chip from her heart. This well-dressed, businesslike stranger bore no resemblance to the Nick she'd fallen in love with.

Nick turned to Donaldson. "I have something to say."

"We've already had this conversation." The man's tone dripped icicles. "The answer is no."

She wasn't imagining it. The tension in the room was palpable.

Nick's smile wasn't pleasant. "Perhaps you'd better look at this before you give me a final answer." He dropped a folder on the desk in front of Donaldson and took a step back. "I'll wait."

Emily exchanged confused looks with Jefferson Wade. The attorney seemed as much at a loss as she was. If Nick had some unfinished business with his boss, couldn't it wait until they'd made their plea?

The contents of the folder had an odd effect on Donaldson. He went first pale, then red. He glared at Nick.

"You can't be serious."

Nick's smile didn't change. "Can't I?"

"What do you intend to do with this pack of nonsense?"

"I think there are several regulatory agencies which might find something of interest there. The newspapers certainly would, to say nothing of the stockholders."

Donaldson's eyes narrowed. "You're committing professional suicide, you know that. Nobody will hire you after this."

Nick's eyebrows lifted and his lips curved in what seemed a more genuine smile. "You won't believe it, but that doesn't matter in the least." His face hardened. "You know what I want."

Emily had a sudden urge to say something, anything, that would break the tension in the room. Wade put his hand on her arm, giving a warning shake of his head.

Donaldson glared at Nick for another long moment. Then he folded the papers together and shoveled them into a briefcase. He turned to Emily.

"Ms. Carmichael, in accordance with Clause 52B of our contract, I am rescinding the agreement to merge Carmichael Mills with Ex Corp. Your attorney will have the pertinent papers by this afternoon.''

He stalked out of the room, and Nick followed him without a backward glance.

Emily stared blankly at the door that had closed behind them. ''I don't understand. What just happened here?''

''You heard him.'' Wade seemed as astonished as she was, but attempting to hide it under a professional manner. ''Ex Corp had the option to back out of the deal, and they've done it.'' A totally unprofessional grin burst through his solemn façade. ''They've backed down. Carmichael Mills is back in business.''

''But...'' She was too stunned to celebrate. ''But why? What did Nick do?''

He shrugged. ''I don't pretend to know what was in those papers he showed Donaldson, but at a guess, I'd say Ex Corp has sailed pretty close to the wind in some of their business dealings. Probably nothing outright illegal, but questionable enough to raise eyebrows and start an investigation if someone in the know started talking.''

''Someone like Nick.'' She was still trying to absorb it all.

He gave her a shrewd look. ''I'd say we owe quite a debt to that young man. Ex Corp isn't likely to forgive and forget, and they won't hesitate to make it hard for anyone else to hire him. Looks as if he's sacrificed his career for this town.'' Wade lifted the telephone. "Do you mind if I let a few people know?"

She shook her head, still trying to process it. Nick had saved them. First he'd betrayed them, and now he'd saved them. How did she make any sense of that?

Nick glanced around the study of the rented house. Funny that it had started to feel so much like home in the brief time he'd been there. Well, no longer. He dumped a few magazines in the trash can, then pulled one out and put it in his briefcase. Might as well have something to read on the plane.

The telephone rang, and he eyed it warily. When he'd come in he'd found several messages on the machine from Emily. Her voice had sounded wary, as if she didn't quite know what to say to him.

He'd already made up his mind that the best thing he could do for Emily and the boys was to leave. He shouldn't even speak to her again. He shouldn't. But he picked up the phone and said, "Hello."

"Hey, buddy." Josh sounded muted, and Nick had a wry image of him glancing over his shoulder and shielding the receiver so no one from Ex Corp would know whom he'd called.

"Hey, yourself. You sure you want to talk to me?"

Josh cleared his throat. "Just wanted to say—well, did you know what you were doing today?"

"I knew." And he knew the cost, too. But somehow, losing his career didn't stack up against the pain of losing Emily again. "How's Donaldson taking it?"

"He doesn't like to lose. I wouldn't count on getting a job anywhere in the industry for a while."

"Don't worry. I'm not." He didn't know what he was going to do, but he knew it wouldn't be something where getting ahead meant trampling on other people.

"Well..." Josh seemed at a loss for words. Nick suspected his actions didn't fit into any frame of reference Josh knew. "I wish you luck, anyway."

He hung up, smiling a little. Josh didn't understand. Maybe he didn't understand all that well himself, but he knew he felt better than he had in a long time.

Thank you, Lord, for showing me what I was. Give me an idea of what I can be.

In the silence, voices floated through the open window.

"Maybe he's not there."

"He must be. The light's on. Go look."

"I'm not going. You go look."

Shaking his head, he went to the window. He should have known they'd come.

"Hi, guys."

They stood side by side in the pool of light from the window, looking up at him. They were so like Emily that his heart ached.

"Hi, Nick." As usual, Trey was the first to speak.

"We wanted to see you. Do you want to come out?" David sounded hopeful.

"I don't think so." He leaned on the windowsill. "I'm pretty busy with stuff."

"About the mill?" Trey asked.

"What do you know about the mill?" What would Emily have told them after that meeting?

"We know you saved the mill."

"Mommy said so."

Something that had been very tight inside him eased at that. "How is your mom?"

Trey wrinkled his nose. "She's been really busy. Lots of people keep calling about the mill, I guess."

David nudged him. "Ask him."

"You ask him."

David lifted his chin. "Okay, I will." He looked at Nick. "Will you stay, Nick? Please? We'd really like it if you would."

Something seemed to have his throat in a vise. He swallowed. "Afraid I can't, guys."

They exchanged glances, communicating in that wordless manner they had.

"Will you talk to Mom before you go?" Trey leaned forward, reaching up to put his hands on the sill. "Will you?"

Nick covered the small hands with his, then leaned down to tousle David's hair. "We'll see."

"That's what Mom said, too." Trey looked as if he were trying to hold on to some hope.

He cleared his throat. "Speaking of your mom, she's probably wondering where you are. Maybe you'd better get on home."

They exchanged glances again. Then they turned and darted off across the darkened lawn.

Emily came slowly awake and blinked at the clock. It was barely 6:00 a.m. What had wakened her so early?

The door to her bedroom burst open and the pajama-clad twins raced into the room.

"Mommy, you have to get up." David tugged at her.

Trey thrust her robe at her. "Hurry, Mom. You have to talk to Nick."

She swung her feet to the floor and took the robe. "Boys, calm down. I told you I'd talk to Nick today." She had to express her thanks, even though the fact that Nick hadn't returned her calls made it clear he didn't have anything to say to her.

"You don't understand!" David's face crinkled as if he were about to burst into tears. "You have to go *now.*"

"I can't…"

"He's going, Mom. We saw him from our window. He's packed the car and he's leaving. You have to stop him."

"Hurry!"

David grabbed one hand and Trey the other. They tugged her toward the door.

"Wait…I have to get dressed."

"You can't wait." David's voice shook with urgency. "He's going right this minute."

"I can't go outside like this! What will people..."

She stopped, hearing her own words ringing in her ears. Knowing she'd said them before, to Nick. Knowing what his response would be. *Still afraid of what people will think, Emily?*

No. She wasn't going to live her life any longer afraid of what people might think about her. She wasn't going to let Nick leave, not until she'd said what she had to say to him.

"All right, hurry!" She grabbed the boys' hands. "Let's go!"

Down the stairs, out the kitchen door, the wet grass soaking the hem of her robe. It didn't matter. It didn't matter how wet she got; it didn't matter if all of Mannington saw her. All that mattered was that she got to Nick before he drove out of her life.

"Nick!" The boys bolted ahead of her. They reached Nick just as he started to back out the driveway.

"Wait!" Trey pounded on the driver's side window. "You have to wait."

Face startled, Nick switched off the ignition. He got out, looking from one twin to the other. "What are you doing...?" Then he looked up and saw her.

She stopped, acutely aware of her tousled hair, wet robe and bare feet. "We were trying to stop you."

"So I see."

There wasn't any expression in his face at all, and her heart sank. He didn't want to see them.

"We want to talk to you." She had to go through with it.

"Look, if you're trying to thank me, you don't need to."

"I think so." She tried to smile. "You saved us."

Pain flickered in his face. "I was the one who put you in jeopardy."

Somehow that instant of pain gave her hope...hope that he wasn't gone from them entirely.

"And then you got us out again. Why, Nick? Why did you sacrifice your career for us?"

He looked at her soberly. "Because I had a look into my soul, and I didn't like what I saw. You were right about me. I was letting revenge turn me into someone not even I could like."

Tears welled in her eyes, and she blinked them back. "And now?"

His gaze slid away from hers. "And now I'd better leave. Before I cause any more damage."

Trey, apparently unable to be still any longer, nudged her. "Ask him, Mommy."

"Ask him," David echoed.

Ask him.

She held out her hand. "Please, Nick. We want you to stay."

For a long moment he didn't move. Then he took a step toward her, blue eyes blazing with hope. "Do you mean it?"

"We mean it."

She moved into his arms, feeling them close around

her, strong and sure. She lifted her face to his kiss. If the entire town of Mannington chose to watch Emily Carmichael in her bathrobe being kissed by Nick O'Neill, she didn't care in the least. God had given them both a second chance at love, and she wouldn't let that love get away ever again.

Epilogue

"Kick it, David!" Emily shouted as the soccer players surged down the field. Maybe he heard her. He kicked, then grinned as the ball sailed into the net.

Trey was the first one to reach him, closely followed by Alison, red hair gleaming in the sun. They pounded him on the back. Next to Emily, baby Lisa lurched forward in her stroller, pounding the tray with her rattle.

Emily dropped a kiss on her daughter's soft black curls. The baby looked more like Nick every day, with those deep blue eyes and blue-black hair. "Your brother made a goal. You cheer."

Lisa gave her a grin that showed her two teeth and pounded the rattle again.

Surely Nick couldn't hear that, but he caught her eye from across the field, and her heart warmed at his look. He turned to exchange high fives with Ken. The two of them had taken over coaching the soccer team this year, and they were even more excited than the kids over every victory.

"Looks like we'll be buying everyone ice cream again tonight," Lorna said. "The traditional victory celebration is getting expensive."

"We can handle it," Emily said, smiling.

Truth to tell, there'd been some difficult times at the mill in the last two years, times when they'd all had to pinch their pennies. But thanks to Nick's wise management, the mill was thriving. His idea to offer a profit-sharing plan to the employees had been pure genius.

Even James had radiated approval from his retirement home in Arizona. Now everyone in Mannington, it seemed, had a stake in how the mill did. It belonged to all of them in a way it never had before, and that had made them a stronger community.

The whistle blew, and Emily watched her three guys come toward them across the field. Her heart filled with love so intense that she had to blink back tears.

Thank you, Lord. Thank you for giving all of us a second chance to do things right.

* * * * *

Dear Reader,

Thank you for reading my Love Inspired novel, *Since You've Been Gone*. I hope you enjoyed the story of Emily's reunion with her first love, Nick, and their triumph over the barriers that kept them apart. I had fun creating the twins, Trey and David, and hope they made you smile.

Forgiveness is one of those lessons I've had to learn over and over in my life, but God keeps giving me another chance to get it right. Perhaps that's true for you, too.

Best Wishes,

Marta Perry